The Blue Moon

Laurence Housman

1ᵉᵗ WORLD
LIBRARY
Literary Society

The Blue Moon

Laurence Housman

© 1st World Library – Literary Society, 2005
PO Box 2211
Fairfield, IA 52556
www.1stworldlibrary.org
First Edition

LCCN: 2004195644

Softcover ISBN: 1-4218-0466-2
Hardcover ISBN: 1-4218-0366-6
eBook ISBN: 1-4218-0566-9

Purchase *"The Blue Moon"*
as a traditional bound book at:
www.1stWorldLibrary.org/purchase.asp?ISBN=1-4218-0466-2

1st World Library Literary Society is a nonprofit
organization dedicated to promoting literacy by:

- Creating a free internet library accessible from any
  computer worldwide.
- Hosting writing competitions and offering book
  publishing scholarships.

The Blue Moon
contributed by Tim, Ed & Rodney
in support of
1st World Library Literary Society

CONTENTS

THE BLUE MOON

Nillywill and Hands-pansy were the most unimportant and happy pair of lovers the world has ever gained or lost.

With them it had been a case of love at first blindness since the day when they had tumbled into each other's arms in the same cradle. And Hands-pansy, when he first saw her, did not discover that Nillywill was a real princess hiding her birthright in the home of a poor peasant; nor did Nillywill, when she first saw Hands, see in him the baby-beginnings of the most honest and good heart that ever sprang out of poverty and humble parentage. So from her end of their little crib she kicked him with her royal rosy toes, and he from his kicked back and laughed: and thus, as you hear, at first blindness they fell head over ears in love with one another.

Nothing could undo that; for day by day earth and sun and wind came to rub it in deeper, and water could not wash it off. So when they had been seven years together there could be no doubt that they felt as if they had been made for each other in heaven. And then something very big and sad came to pass; for one day Nillywill had to leave off being a peasant child and become a princess once more. People very grand and grown-up came to the woodside where she flowered so gaily, and caught her by the golden hair of her head and pulled her up by her dear little roots, and carried her quite away from Hands-pansy to a place she had never been in before. They put her into a large palace, with woods and terraces and landscape gardens on all sides of it; and there she sat crying and pale, saying that she wanted to be taken back to Hands-pansy and grow up and marry him, though he was but the poor peasant boy he had always been.

Those that had charge of Nillywill in her high station talked wisely, telling her to forget him. "For," said they, "such a thing as a princess marrying a peasant boy can only happen once in a blue moon!"

When she heard that, Nillywill began every night to watch the moon rise, hoping some evening to see it grow up like a blue flower against the dusk and shake down her wish to her like a bee out of its deep bosom.

But night by night, silver, or ruddy, or primrose, it lit a place for itself in the heavens; and years went by, bringing the Princess no nearer to her desire to find room for Hands-pansy amid the splendours of her throne.

She knew that he was five thousand miles away and had only wooden peasant shoes to walk in; and when she begged that she might once more have sight of him, her whole court, with the greatest utterable politeness, cried "No!"

The Princess's memory sang to her of him in a thousand tunes, like woodland birds carolling; but it was within the cage which men call a crown that her thoughts moved, fluttering to be out of it and free.

Laurence Housman

So time went on, and Nillywill had entered gently into sweet womanhood - the comeliest princess that ever dropped a tear; and all she could do for love was to fill her garden with dark-eyed pansies, and walk among their humble upturned faces which reminded her so well of her dear Hands - Hands who was a long five thousand miles away. "And, oh !" she sighed, watching for the blue moon to rise, "when will it come and make me at one with all my wish?"

Looking up, she used to wonder what went on there. She and Hands had stolen into the woods, when children together, and watched the small earth-fairies at play, and had seen them, when the moon was full, lift up their arms to it, making, perhaps, signals of greeting to far-off moon-brothers. So she thought to herself, "What kind are the fairies up there, and who is the greatest moon-fairy of all who makes the blue moon rise and bring good-will to the sad wishers of the human race? Is it," thought Nillywill, "the moon-fairy who then opens its heart and brings down healing therefrom to lovers upon earth?"

And now, as happens to all those who are captives of a crown, Nillywill learned that she must wed with one of her own rank who was a stranger to her save for his name and his renown as the lord of a neighbouring country; there was no help for her, since she was a princess, but she must wed according to the claims of her station. When she heard of it, she went at nightfall to her pansies, all lying in their beds, and told them of her grief. They, awakened by her tears, lifted up their grave eyes and looked at her.

"Do you not hear?" said they.

"Hear what?" asked the Princess.

"We are low in the ground: we hear!" said the pansies. "Stoop down your head and listen!"

The Princess let her head go to the ground; and "click, click," she heard wooden shoes coming along the road. She ran to the gate, and there was Hands, tall and lean, dressed as a poor peasant, with a bundle tied up in a blue cotton handkerchief across his shoulder, and five thousand miles trodden to nothing by the faithful tramping of his old wooden shoes.

"Oh, the blue moon, the blue moon!" cried the Princess; and running down the road, she threw herself into his arms.

How happy and proud they were of each other! He, because she remembered him and knew him so well by the sight of his face and the sound of his feet after all these years; and she, because he had come all that way in a pair of wooden shoes, just as he was, and had not been afraid that she would be ashamed to know him again.

"I am so hungry!" said Hands, when he and Nillywill had done kissing each other. And when Nillywill heard that, she brought him into the palace through the pansies by her own private way; then with her own hands she set food before him, and made him eat. Hands, looking at her, said, "You are quite as beautiful as I thought you would be!"

"And you - so are you!" she answered, laughing and clapping her hands. And "Oh, the blue moon," she cried - "surely the blue moon must rise to-night!"

Laurence Housman

Low down in the west the new moon, leaning on its side, rocked and turned softly in its sleep; and there, facing the earth through the cleared night, the blue moon hung like a burning grape against the sky. Like the heart of a sapphire laid open, the air flushed and purpled to a deeper shade. The wind drew in its breath close and hushed, till not a leaf quaked in the boughs; and the sea that lay out west gathered its waves together softly to its heart, and let the heave of its tide fall wholly to slumber. Round-eyed, the stars looked at themselves in the charmed water, while in a luminous azure flood the light of the blue moon flowed abroad.

Under the light of many tapers within drawn curtains of tapestry, and feasting her eyes upon the happiness of Hands, the Princess felt the change that had entranced the outer world. "I feel," she said, "I do not know how - as if the palace were standing siege. Come out where we can breathe the fresh air!"

The light of the tapers grew ghostly and dim, as, parting the thick hangings of the window, they stepped into the night.

"The blue moon!" cried Nillywill to her heart; "oh, Hands, it is the blue moon!"

All the world seemed carved out of blue stone; trees with stems dark-veined as marble rose up to give rest to boughs which drooped the altered hues of their foliage like the feathers of peacocks at roost. Jewel within jewel they burned through every shade from blue to onyx. The white blossoms of a cherry-tree had become changed into turquoise, and the tossing spray of a fountain as it drifted and swung was like a column of blue fire. Where a long inlet of sea reached in and touched the feet of the hanging gardens the stars showed like glow-worms, emerald in a floor of amethyst.

There was no motion abroad, nor sound: even the voice of the nightingale was stilled, because the passion of his desire had become visible before his eyes.

"Once in a blue moon!" said Nilly-will, waiting for her dream to become altogether true. "Let us go now, she said, "where I can put away my crown! To-night has brought you to me, and the blue moon has come for us: let us go!"

"Where shall we go?" asked Hands.

"As far as we can," cried Nillywill. "Suppose to the blue moon! To-night it seems as if one might tread on water or air. Yonder across the sea, with the stars for stepping-stones, we might get to the blue moon as it sets into the waves."

But as they went through the deep alleys of the garden that led down to the shore they came to a sight more wonderful than anything they had yet seen.

Before them, facing toward the sea, stood two great reindeer, their high horns reaching to the overhead boughs; and behind them lay a sledge, long and with deep sides like the sides of a ship. All blue they seemed in that strange light.

There too, but nearer to hand, was the moon-fay himself waiting - a great figure of lofty stature, clad in furs of blue fox-skin, and with heron's wings fastened above the flaps of his hood; and these lifted themselves and clapped as Hands and the Princess drew near.

"Are you coming to the blue moon ?" called the fay, and his voice whistled and shrewed to them like the voice of a wind.

Hands-pansy gave back answer stoutly: "Yes, yes, we are coming!" And indeed what better could he say?

"But," cried Nillywill, holding back for a moment, "what will the blue moon do for us?"

"Once you are there," answered the moon-fay, "you can have your wish and your heart's desire; but only once in a blue moon can you have it. Are you coming?"

"We are coming!" cried Nillywill. "Oh, let us make haste!"

"Tread softly," whispered the moon-fay, "and stoop well under these boughs, for if anything awakes to behold the blue moon, the memory of it can never die. On earth only the nightingale of all living things has beheld a blue moon; and the triumph and pain of that memory wakens him ever since to sing all night long. Tread softly, lest others waken and learn to cry after us; for we in the blue moon have our sleep troubled by those who cry for a blue moon to return." He looked towards Nillywill, and smiled with friendly eyes. "Come!" he said again, and all at once they had leapt upon the sledge, and the reindeer were running fast down toward the sea.

The blue moon was resting with its lower rim upon the

waters. At that sight, before they were clear of the avenues of the garden, one of the reindeer tossed up his great branching horns and snorted aloud for joy. With a soft stir in the thick boughs overhead, a bird with a great trail of feathers moved upon its perch.

The sledge, gliding from land, passed out over the smoothed waters, running swiftly as upon ice; and the reflection of the stars shone up like glow-worms as Nillywill and Hands-pansy, in the moon-fay's company, sped away along its bright surface.

The still air whistled through the reindeers' horns; so fast they went that the trees and the hanging gardens and the palace walls melted away from view like wreaths of smoke. Sky and sea became one magic sapphire drawing them in towards the centre of its life, to the heart of the blue moon itself.

When the blue moon had set below the sea, then far behind upon the land they had left the leaves rustled and drew themselves sharply together, shuddering to get rid of the stony stillness, and the magic hues in which they had been dyed; and again the nightingale broke out into passionate triumph and complaint.

Then also from the bough which the reindeer had brushed with its horns a peacock threw back its head and cried in harsh lamentation, having no sweet voice wherewith to acclaim its prize. And so ever since it cries, as it goes up into the boughs to roost, because it shares with the nightingale its grief for the memory of departed beauty which never returns to earth save once in a blue moon.

But Nillywill and Hands-pansy, living together in the

Laurence Housman

blue moon, look back upon the world, if now and then they choose to remember, without any longing for it or sorrow.

A CHINESE FAIRY TALE

Tiki-pu was a small grub of a thing; but he had a true love of Art deep down in his soul. There it hung mewing and complaining, struggling to work its way out through the raw exterior that bound it.

Tiki-pu s master professed to be an artist: he had apprentices and students, who came daily to work under him, and a large studio littered about with the performances of himself and his pupils. On the walls hung also a few real works by the older men, all long since dead.

This studio Tiki-pu swept; for those who worked in it he ground colours, washed brushes, and ran errands, bringing them their dog chops and bird's-nest soup from the nearest eating-house whenever they were too busy to go out to it themselves. He himself had to feed mainly on the breadcrumbs which the students screwed into pellets for their drawings and then threw about upon the floor. It was on the floor, also, that he had to sleep at night.

Tiki-pu looked after the blinds, and mended the paper window-panes, which were often broken when the apprentices threw their brushes and mahl-sticks at him. Also he strained rice-paper over the linen-stretchers, ready for the painters to work on; and for a treat, now

Laurence Housman

and then, a lazy one would allow him to mix a colour for him. Then it was that Tiki-pu's soul came down into his finger-tips, and his heart beat so that he gasped for joy. Oh, the yellows and the greens, and the lakes and the cobalts, and the purples which sprang from the blending of them! Sometimes it was all he could do to keep himself from crying out.

Tiki-pu, while he squatted and ground at the colour-powders, would listen to his master lecturing to the students. He knew by heart the names of all the painters and their schools, and the name of the great leader of them all who had lived and passed from their midst more than three hundred years ago; he knew that too, a name like the sound of the wind, Wio-wani: the big picture at the end of the studio was by him.

That picture! To Tiki-pu it seemed worth all the rest of the world put together. He knew, too, the story which was told of it, making it as holy to his eyes as the tombs of his own ancestors. The apprentices joked over it, calling it "Wio-wani's back-door," "Wio-wani's night-cap," and many other nicknames; but Tiki-pu was quite sure, since the picture was so beautiful, that the story must be true.

Wio-wani, at the end of a long life, had painted it; a garden full of trees and sunlight, with high-standing flowers and green paths, and in their midst a palace. "The place where I would like to rest," said Wio-wani, when it was finished.

So beautiful was it then, that the Emperor himself had come to see it; and gazing enviously at those peaceful walks, and the palace nestling among the trees, had sighed and owned that he too would be glad of such a resting-place. Then Wio-wani stepped into the picture, and walked away along a path till he came, looking quite small and far-off, to a low door in the palace-wall. Opening it, he turned and beckoned to the Emperor; but the Emperor did not follow; so Wio-wani went in by himself, and shut the door between himself and the world for ever.

That happened three hundred years ago; but for Tiki-pu the story was as fresh and true as if it had happened yesterday. When he was left to himself in the studio, all alone and locked up for the night, Tiki-pu used to go and stare at the picture till it was too dark to see, and at the little palace with the door in its wall by which Wio-wani had disappeared out of life. Then his soul would go down into his finger-tips, and he would knock softly and fearfully at the beautifully painted door, saying, "Wio-wani, are you there?"

Little by little in the long-thinking nights, and the slow early mornings when light began to creep back through the papered windows of the studio, Tiki-pu's soul became too much for him. He who could strain paper, and grind colours, and wash brushes, had everything within reach for becoming an artist, if it was the will of fate that he should be one.

He began timidly at first, but in a little while he grew bold. With the first wash of light he was up from his couch on the hard floor, and was daubing his soul out on scraps, and odds-and-ends, and stolen pieces of rice-paper.

Before long the short spell of daylight which lay between dawn and the arrival of the apprentices to their work did not suffice him. It took him so long to

Laurence Housman

hide all traces of his doings, to wash out the brushes, and rinse clean the paint-pots he had used, and on the top of that to get the studio swept and dusted, that there was hardly time left him in which to indulge the itching appetite in his fingers.

Driven by necessity, he became a pilferer of candleÄends, picking them from their sockets in the lanterns which the students carried on dark nights. Now and then one of these would remember that, when last used, his lantern had had a candle in it, and would accuse Tiki-pu of having stolen it. "It is true," he would confess ; "I was hungry - I have eaten it." The lie was so probable, he was believed easily, and was well beaten accordingly. Down in the ragged linings of his coat Tiki-pu could hear the candle-ends rattling as the buffeting and chastisement fell upon him, and often he trembled lest his hoard should be discovered. But the truth of the matter never leaked out and at night, as soon as he guessed that all the world outside was in bed, Tiki-pu would mount one of his candles on a wooden stand and paint by the light of it, blinding himself over his task, till the dawn came and gave him a better and cheaper light to work by.

Tiki-pu quite hugged himself over the results; he believed he was doing very well. "If only Wio-wani were here to teach me," thought he, "I would be in the way of becoming a great painter!"

The resolution came to him one night that Wio-wani should teach him. So he took a large piece of rice-paper and strained it, and sitting down opposite "Wio-wani's back-door," began painting. He had never set himself so big a task as this; by the dim stumbling light of his candle he strained his eyes nearly blind over the difficulties of it; and at last was almost driven to despair. How the trees stood row behind row, with air and sunlight between, and how the path went in and out, winding its way up to the little door in the palace-wall were mysteries he could not fathom. He peered and peered and dropped tears into his paint-pots; but the secret of the mystery of such painting was far beyond him.

The door in the palace-wall opened; out came a little old man and began walking down the pathway towards him.

The soul of Tiki-pu gave a sharp leap in his grubby little body. "That must be Wio-wani himself and no other!" cried his soul.

Tiki-pu pulled off his cap and threw himself down on the floor with reverent grovellings. When he dared to look up again Wio-wani stood over him big and fine; just within the edge of his canvas he stood and reached out a hand.

"Come along with me, Tiki-pu!" said the great one. "If you want to know how to paint I will teach you."

"Oh, Wio-wani, were you there all the while?" cried Tiki-pu ecstatically, leaping up and clutching with his smeary little puds the hand which the old man extended to him.

"I was there," said Wio-wani, "looking at you out of my little window. Come along in!"

Tiki-pu took a heave and swung himself into the picture, and fairy capered when he found his feet

Laurence Housman

among the flowers of Wio-wani's beautiful garden. Wio-wani had turned, and was ambling gently back to the door of his palace, beckoning to the small one to follow him; and there stood Tiki-pu, opening his mouth like a fish to all the wonders that surrounded him. "Celestiality, may I speak?" he said suddenly.

"Speak," replied Wio-wani; "what is it?"

"The Emperor, was he not the very flower of fools not to follow when you told him?"

"I cannot say," answered Wio-wani, "but he certainly was no artist."

Then he opened the door, that door which he had so beautifully painted, and led Tiki-pu in. And outside the little candle-end sat and guttered by itself, till the wick fell overboard, and the flame kicked itself out, leaving the studio in darkness and solitude to wait for the growings of another dawn.

It was full day before Tiki-pu re- appeared; he came running down the green path in great haste, jumped out of the frame on to the studio floor, and began tidying up his own messes of the night and the apprentices' of the previous day. Only just in time did he have things ready by the hour when his master and the others returned to their work.

All that day they kept scratching their left ears, and could not think why; but Tiki-pu knew, for he was saying over to himself all the things that Wio-wani, the great painter, had been saying about them and their precious productions. And as he ground their colours for them and washed their brushes, and filled his famished little body with the breadcrumbs they threw away, little they guessed from what an immeasurable distance he looked down upon them all, and had Wio-wani's word for it tickling his right ear all the day long.

Now before long Tiki-pu's master noticed a change in him; and though he bullied him, and thrashed him, and did all that a careful master should do, he could not get the change out of him. So in a short while he grew suspicious. "What is the boy up to?" he wondered. "I have my eye on him all day: it must be at night that he gets into mischief."

It did not take Tiki-pu's master a night's watching to find that something surreptitious was certainly going on. When it was dark he took up his post outside the studio, to see whether by any chance Tiki-pu had some way of getting out; and before long he saw a faint light showing through the window. So he came and thrust his finger softly through one of the panes, and put his eye to the hole.

There inside was a candle burning on a stand, and Tiki-pu squatting with paint-pots and brush in front of Wio-Wani's last masterpiece.

"What fine piece of burglary is this?" thought he; "what serpent have I been harbouring in my bosom? Is this beast of a grub of a boy thinking to make himself a painter and cut me out of my reputation and prosperity?" For even at that distance he could perceive plainly that the work of this boy went head and shoulders beyond his, or that of any painter then living.

Presently Wio-wani opened his door and came down the path, as was his habit now each night, to call Tiki-

Laurence Housman

pu to his lesson. He advanced to the front of his picture and beckoned for Tiki-pu to come in with him; and Tiki-pu's master grew clammy at the knees as he beheld Tiki-pu catch hold of Wio-wani's hand and jump into the picture, and skip up the green path by Wio-wani's side, and in through the little door that Wio-wani had painted so beautifully in the end wall of his palace!

For a time Tiki-pu's master stood glued to the spot with grief and horror. "Oh, you deadly little underling! Oh, you poisonous little caretaker, you parasite, you vampire, you fly in amber!" cried he, "is that where you get your training? Is it there that you dare to go trespassing; into a picture that I purchased for my own pleasure and profit, and not at all for yours? Very soon we will see whom it really belongs to!"

He ripped out the paper of the largest window-pane and pushed his way through into the studio. Then in great haste he took up paint-pot and brush, and sacrilegiously set himself to work upon Wio-wani's last masterpiece. In the place of the doorway by which Tiki-pu had entered he painted a solid brick wall; twice over he painted it, making it two bricks thick; brick by brick he painted it, and mortared every brick to its place. And when he had quite finished he laughed, and called "Good-night, Tiki-pu!" and went home to bed quite happy.

The next day all the apprentices were wondering what had become of Tiki-pu; but as the master himself said nothing, and as another boy came to act as colour-grinder and brush-washer to the establishment, they very soon forgot all about him.

In the studio the master used to sit at work with his students all about him, and a mind full of ease and contentment. Now and then he would throw a glance across to the bricked-up doorway of Wio-wani's palace, and laugh to himself, thinking how well he had served out Tiki-pu for his treachery and presumption.

One day - it was five years after the disappearance of Tiki-pu - he was giving his apprentices a lecture on the glories and the beauties and the wonders of Wio-wani's painting - how nothing for colour could excel, or for mystery could equal it. To add point to his eloquence, he stood waving his hallds before Wio-wani's last masterpiece, and all his students and apprentices sat round him and looked.

Suddenly he stopped at mid-word, and broke off in the full flight of his eloquence, as he saw something like a hand come and take down the top brick from the face of paint which he had laid over the little door in the palace-wall which Wio-wani had so beautifully painted. In another moment there was no doubt about it; brick by brick the wall was being pulled down, in spite of its double thickness.

The lecturer was altogether too dumfounded and terrified to utter a word. He and all his apprentices stood round and stared while the demolition of the wall proceeded. Before long he recognised Wio-wani with his flowing white beard; it was his handiwork, this pulling down of the wall! He still had a brick in his hand when he stepped through the opening that he had made, and close after him stepped Tiki-pu!

Tiki-pu was grown tall and strong - he was even handsome; but for all that his old master recognised him, and saw with an envious foreboding that under his arms he carried many rolls and stretchers and portfolios, and other belongings of his craft. Clearly Tiki-pu was coming back into the world, and was going to be a great painter.

Down the garden-path came Wio-wani, and Tiki-pu walked after him; Tiki-pu was so tall that his head stood well over Wio-wani's shoulders - old man and young man together made a handsome pair.

How big Wio-wani grew as he walked down the avenues of his garden and into the foreground of his picture! and how big the brick in his hand! and ah, how angry he seemed!

Wio-wani came right down to the edge of the picture-frame and held up the brick. "What did you do that for?" he asked.

"I . . . didn't!" Tiki-pu's old master was beginning to reply; and the lie was still rolling on his tongue when the weight of the brick-bat, hurled by the stout arm of Wio-wani, felled him. After that he never spoke again. That brick-bat, which he himself had reared, became his own tombstone.

Just inside the picture-frame stood Tiki-pu, kissing the wonderful hands of Wio-wani, which had taught him all their skill. "Good-bye, Tiki-pu!" said Wio-wani, embracing him tenderly. "Now I am sending my second self into the world. When you are tired and want rest come back to me: old Wio-wani will take you in."

Tiki-pu was sobbing, and the tears were running down

his cheeks as he stepped out of Wio-wani's wonder-fully painted garden and stood once more upon earth. Turning, he saw the old man walking away along the path toward the little door under the palace-wall. At the door Wio-wani turned back and waved his hand for the last time. Tiki-pu still stood watching him. Then the door opened and shut, and Wio-wani was gone. Softly as a flower the picture seemed to have folded its leaves over him.

Tiki-pu leaned a wet face against the picture and kissed the door in the palace-wall which Wio-wani had painted so beautifully. "O Wio-wani, dear master," he cried, "are you there?"

He waited, and called again, but no voice answered him.

Laurence Housman

THE WAY OF THE WIND

Where the world breaks up into islands among the blue waves of an eastern sea, in a little house by the seashore, lived Katipah, the only child of poor parents. When they died she was left quite alone and could not find a heart in the world to care for her. She was so poor that no man thought of marrying her, and so delicate and small that as a drudge she was worth nothing to anybody.

Once a month she would go and stand at the shrine gate, and say to the people as they went in to pray, "Will nobody love me?" And the people would turn their heads away quickly and make haste to get past, and in their hearts would wonder to themselves: "Foolish little Katipah! Does she think that we can spare time to love any one so poor and unprofitable as she?"

On the other days Katipah would go down to the beach, where everybody went who had a kite to fly - for all the men in that country flew kites, and all the children, - and there she would fly a kite of her own up into the blue air; and watching the wind carrying it farther and farther away, would grow quite happy thinking how a day might come at last when she would really be loved, though her queer little outside made her seem so poor and unprofitable.

Katipah's kite was green, with blue eyes in its square face; and in one corner it had a very small pursed-up red mouth holding a spray of peach-blossom. She had made it herself; and to her it meant the green world, with the blue sky over it when the spring begins to be sweet, and there, tucked away in one corner of it, her own little warm mouth waiting and wishing to be kissed: and out of all that wishing and waiting the blossom of hope was springing, never to be let go.

All round her were hundreds of others flying their kites, and all had some wish or prayer to Fortune. But Katipah's wish and prayer were only that she might be loved.

The silver sandhills lay in loops and chains round the curve of the blue bay, and all along them flocks of gaily coloured kites hovered and fluttered and sprang. And, as they went up into the clear air, the wind sighing in the strings was like the crying of a young child. "Wahoo! wahoo!" every kite seemed to cradle the wailings of an invisible infant as it went mounting aloft, spreading its thin apron to the wind.

"Wahoo! wahoo!" sang Katipah's blue-and-green kite, "shall I ever be loved by anybody?" And Katipah, keeping fast hold of the string, would watch where it mounted and looked so small, and think that surely some day her kite would bring her the only thing she much cared about.

Katipah's next-door neighbour had everything that her own lonely heart most wished for: not only had she a husband, but a fine baby as well. Yet she was such a jealous, cross-grained body that she seemed to get no happiness out of the fortune Heaven had sent her.

　　　　　　　Laurence Housman

Husband and child seemed both to have caught the infection of her bitter temper: all day and night beating and brawling went on; there seemed no peace in that house.

But for all that the woman, whose name was Bimsha, was quite proud of being a wife and a mother: and in the daytime, when her man was away, she would look over the fence and laugh at Katipah, crying boastfully, "Don't think you will ever have a husband, Katipah: you are too poor and unprofitable! Look at me, and be envious!"

Then Katipah would go softly away, and send up her kite by the seashore till she heard a far-off, sweet, babe-like cry as the wind blew through the strings high in air.

"Shall I ever be loved by anybody?" thought she, as she jerked at the cord; and away the kite flew higher than ever, and the sound of its call grew fainter.

One morning, in the beginning of the year, Katipah went up on to the hill under plum-boughs white with bloom, meaning to gather field-sorrel for her midday meal; and as she stooped with all her hair blowing over her face, and her skirts knotting and billowing round her pretty brown ankles, she felt as if some one had kissed her from behind.

"That cannot be," thought Katipah, with her fingers fast upon a stalk of field-sorrel; "it is too soon for anything so good to happen." So she picked the sorrel quietly, and put it into her basket. But now, not to be mistaken, arms came round her, and she was kissed.

She stood up and put her hands into her breast, quite afraid lest her little heart, which had grown so light, should be caught by a puff of wind and blown right away out of her bosom, and over the hill and into the sea, and be drowned.

And now her eyes would not let her doubt; there by her side stood a handsome youth, with quick-fluttering, posy-embroidered raiment. His long dark hair was full of white plum-blossoms, as though he had just pushed his head through the branches above. His hands also were loaded with the same, and they kept sifting out of his long sleeves whenever he moved his arms. Under the hem of his robe Katipah could see that he had heron's wings bound about his ankles.

"He must be very good," thought Katipah, "to be so beautiful! and indeed he must be very good to kiss poor me!"

"Katipah," said the wonderful youth, "though you do not know me, I know you. It is I who so often helped you to fly your green kite by the shore. I have been up there, and have looked into its blue eyes, and kissed its little red mouth which held the peach-blossom. It was I who made songs in its strings for your heart to hear. I am the West Wind, Katipah - the wind that brings fine weather. 'Gamma-gata' you must call me, for it is I who bring back the wings that fly till the winter is over. And now I have come down to earth, to fetch you away and make you my wife. Will you come, Katipah?"

"I will come, Gamma-gata!" said Katipah, and she crouched and kissed the heron-wings that bound his feet; then she stood up and let herself go into his arms.

Laurence Housman

"Have you enough courage?" asked the West Wind.

"I do not know," answered Katipah, "for I have never tried."

"To come with me," said the Wind, "you need to have much courage; if you have not, you must wait till you learn it. But none the less for that shall you be the wife of Gamma-gata, for I am the gate of the wild geese, as my name says, and my heart is foolish with love of you." Gamma-gata took her up in his arms, and swung with her this way and that, tossing his way through blossom and leaf; and the sunlight became an eddy of gold round her, and wind and laughter seemed to become part of her being, so that she was all giddy and dazed and glad when at last Gamma-gata set her down.

"Stand still, my little one!" he cried - "stand still while I put on your bridal veil for you; then your blushes shall look like a rose-bush in snow!" So Katipah stood with her feet in the green sorrel, and Gamma-gata went up into the plum-tree and shook, till from head to foot she was showered with white blossom.

"How beautiful you seem to me!" cried Gamma-gata when he returned to ground.

Then he lifted her once more and set her in the top of a plum-tree, and going below, cried up to her, "Leap, little Wind-wife, and let me see that you have courage!"

Katipah looked long over the deep space that lay between them, and trembled. Then she fixed her eyes fast upon those of her lover, and leapt, for in the laughter of his eyes she had lost all her fear.

He caught her halfway in air as she fell. "You are not really brave," said he; "if I had shut my eyes you would not have jumped."

"If you had shut your eyes just then," cried Katipah, "I would have died for fear."

He set her once more in the treetop, and disappeared from her sight. "Come down to me, Katipah!" she heard his voice calling all round her.

Clinging fast to the topmost bough, "Oh, Gamma-gata," she cried, "let me see your eyes, and I will come."

Then with darkened brow he appeared to her again out of his blasts, and took her in his arms and lifted her down a little sadly till her feet touched safe earth. And he blew away the beautiful veil of blossoms with which he had showered her, while Katipah stood like a shamed child and watched it go, shredding itself to pieces in the spring sunshine.

And Gamma-gata, kissing her tenderly, said: "Go home, Katipah, and learn to have courage! and when you have learned it I will be faithful and will return to you again. Only remember, however long we may be parted, and whatever winds blow ill-fortune up to your door, Gamma-gata will watch over you. For in deed and truth you are the wife of the West Wind now, and truly he loves you, Katipah!"

"Oh, Gamma-gata l" cried Katipah, "tell the other winds, when they come, to blow courage into me, and to blow me back to you; and do not let that be long!"

"I will tell them," said Gamma-gata; and suddenly he was gone. Katipah saw a drift of white petals borne over the treetops and away to sea, and she knew that there went Gamma-gata, the beautiful windy youth who, loving her so well, had made her his wife between the showers of the plum-blossom and the sunshine, and had promised to return to her as soon as she was fit to receive him.

So Katipah gathered up her field-sorrel, and went away home and ate her solitary midday meal with a mixture of pride and sorrow in her timid little breast. "Some day, when I am grown brave," she thought, "Gamma-gata will come back to me; but he will not come yet."

In the evening Bimsha looked over the fence and jeered at her. "Do not think, Katipah," she cried, "that you will ever get a husband, for all your soft looks! You are too poor and unprofitable."

Katipah folded her meek little body together like a concertina when it shuts, and squatted to earth in great contentment of spirit. "Silly Bimsha," said she, "I already have a husband, a fine one! Ever so much finer than yours!"

Bimsha turned pale and cold with envy to hear her say that, for she feared that Katipah was too good and simple to tell her an untruth, even in mockery. But she put a brave face upon the matter, saying only, "I will believe in that fine husband of yours when I see him!"

"Oh, you will see him," answered Katipah, "if you look high enough! But he is far away over your head, Bimsha; and you will not hear him beating me at night, for that is not his way!"

At this soft answer Bimsha went back into her house in a fury, and Katipah laughed to herself. Then she sighed, and said, "Oh, Gamma-gata, return to me quickly, lest my word shall seem false to Bimsha, who hates me!"

Every day after this Bimsha thrust her face over the fence to say: "Katipah, where is this fine husband of yours? He does not seem to come home often."

Katipah answered slily; "He comes home late, when it is dark, and he goes away very early, almost before it is light. It is not necessary for his happiness that he should see *you*."

"Certainly there is a change in Katipah," thought Bimsha: "she has become saucy with her tongue." But her envious heart would not allow her to let matters be. Night and morning she cried to Katipah, "Katipah, where is your fine husband?" And Katipah laughed at her, thinking to herself: "To begin with, I will not be afraid of anything Bimsha may say. Let Gamma-gata know that!"

And now every day she looked up into the sky to see what wind was blowing; but east, or north, or south, it was never the one wind that she looked for. The east wind came from the sea, bringing rain, and beat upon Katipah's door at night. Then Katipah would rise and open, and standing in the downpour, would cry, "East wind, east wind, go and tell your brother Gamma-gata that I am not afraid of you any more than I am of Bimsha!"

One night the east wind, when she said that, pulled a tile off Bimsha's house, and threw it at her; and

Laurence Housman

Katipah ran in and hid behind the door in a great hurry. After that she had less to say when the east wind came and blew under her gable and rattled at her door. "Oh, Gamma-gata," she sighed, "if I might only set eyes on you, I would fear nothing at all!"

When the weather grew fine again Katipah returned to the shore and flew her kite as she had always done before the love of Gamma-gata had entered her heart. Now and then, as she did so, the wind would change softly, and begin blowing from the west. Then little Katipah would pull lovingly at the string, and cry, "Oh, Gamma-gata, have you got fast hold of it up there?"

One day after dusk, when she, the last of all the flyers, hauled down her kitc to earth, there she found a heron's feather fastened among the strings. Katipah knew who had sent that, and kissed it a thousand times over; nor did she mind for many days afterwards what Bimsha might say, becausc the heron's feather lay so close to her heart, warming it with the hope of Gamma-gata's return.

But as weeks and months passed on, and Bimsha still did not fail to say each morning, "Katipah, where is your fine husband to-day?" the timid heart grew faint with waiting. "Alas!" thought Katipah, "if Heaven would only send me a child, I would show it to her; she would believe me easily then! However tiny, it would be big enough to convince her. Gamma-gata, it is a very little thing that I ask!"

And now every day and all day long she sent up her kite from the seashore, praying that a child might be born to her and convince Bimsha of the truth. Every one said: "Katipah is mad about kite-flying! See how early she goes and how late she stays: hardly any weather keeps her indoors."

One day the west wind came full-breathed over land and sea, and Katipah was among the first on the beach to send up her messenger with word to Gamma-gata of the thing for which she prayed. "Gamma-gata," she sighed, "the voice of Bimsha afflicts me daily; my heart is bruised by the mockery she casts at me. Did I not love thee under the plum-tree, Gamma-gata? Ask of Heaven, therefore, that a child may be born to me - ever so small let it be - and Bimsha will become dumb. Gamma-gata, it is a very little thing that I am asking!"

All day long she let her kite go farther up into the sky than all the other kites. Overhead the wind sang in their strings like bees, or like the thin cry of very small children; but Katipah's was so far away she could scarcely see it against the blue. "Gamma-gata," she cried; till the twilight drew sea and land together, and she was left alone.

Then she called down her kite sadly; hand over hand she drew it by the cord, till she saw it fluttering over her head like a great moth searching for a flower in the gloom. "Wahoo! wahoo!" she could hear the wind crying through its strings like the wailing of a very small child.

It had become so dark that Katipah hardly knew what the kite had brought her till she touched the tiny warm limbs that lay cradled among the strings that netted the frame to its cord. Full of wonder and delight, she lifted the windling out of its nest, and laid it in her bosom. Then she slung her kite across her shoulder, and ran home, laughing and crying for joy and triumph to think

Laurence Housman

that all Bimsha's mockery must now be at an end. So, quite early the next morning, Katipah sat herself down very demurely in the doorway, with her child hidden in the folds of her gown, and waited for Bimsha's evil eye to look out upon her happiness.

She had not long to wait. Bimsha came out of her door, and looking across to Katipah, cried, "Well, Katipah, and where is your fine husband to-day?"

"My husband is gone out," said Katipah, "but if you care to look you can see my baby. It is ever so much more beautiful than yours."

Bimsha, when she heard that, turned green and yellow with envy; and there, plain to see, was Katipah holding up to view the most beautiful babe that ever gave the sunlight a good excuse for visiting this wicked earth. The mere sight of so much innocent beauty and happiness gave Bimsha a shock from which it took her three weeks to recover. After that she would sit at her window and for pure envy keep watch to see Katipah and the child playing together - the child which was so much more beautiful and well-behaved than her own.

As for Katipah, she was so happy now that the sorrow of waiting for her husband's return grew small. Day by day the west wind blew softly, and she knew that Gamma-gata was there, keeping watch over her and her child.

Every day she would say to the little one, "Come, my plum-petal, my wind-flower, I will send thee up to thy father that he may see how fat thou art getting, and be proud of thee!" And going down to the shore, she would lay the child among the strings of her kite and send it up to where Gamma-gata blew a wide breath over sea and land. As it went she would hear the child crow with joy at being so uplifted from earth, and laughing to herself, she would think, "When he sees his child so patterned after his own heart, Gamma-gata will be too proud to remain long away from me."

When she drew the child back to her out of the sky, she covered it with caresses, crying, "Oh, my wind-blown one, my cloudlet, my sky-blossom, my little piece out of heaven, hast thou seen thy father, and has he told thee that he loves me?" And the child would crow with mysterious delight, being too young to tell anything it knew in words.

Bimsha, out of her window, watched and saw all this, not comprehending it: and in her evil heart a wish grew up that she might by some means put an end to all Katipah's happiness. So one day towards evening, when Katipah, alone upon the shore, had let her kite and her little one go up to the fleecy edges of a cloud through which the golden sunlight was streaming, Bimsha came softly behind and with a sharp knife cut the string by which alone the kite was held from falling.

"Oh, silly Bimsha!" cried Katipah, "what have you done that for?"

Up in air the kite made a far plunge forward, fluttered and stumbled in its course, and came shooting head-long to earth. "Oh dear!" cried Katipah, "it my beautiful little kite gets torn, Bimsha, that will be your fault!"

When the kite fell, it lay unhurt on one of the soft

Laurence Housman

sandhills that ringed the bay; but no sign of the child was to be seen. Katipah was laughing when she picked up her kite and ran home. And Bimsha thought, "Is it witchcraft, or did the child fall into the sea?"

In the night the West Wind came and tapped at Katipah's window; and rising from her bed, she heard Gamma-gata's voice calling tenderly to her. When she opened the window to the blindness of the black night, he kissed her, and putting the little one in her arms, said, "Wait only a little while longer, Katipah, and I will come again to you. Already you are learning to be brave."

In the morning Bimsha looked out, and there sat Katipah in her own doorway, with the child safe and sound in her arms. And, plain to see, he had on a beautiful golden coat, and little silver wings were fastened to his feet, and his head was garnished with a wreath of flowers the like of which were never seen on earth. He was like a child of noble birth and fortune, and the small motherly face of Katipah shone with pride and happiness as she nursed him.

"Where did you steal those things?" asked Bimsha, "and how did that child come back? I thought he had fallen into the sea and been drowned."

"Ah!" answered Katipah slily, "he was up in the clouds when the kite left him, and he came down with the rain last night. It is nothing wonderful. You were foolish, Bimsha, if you thought that to fall into the clouds would do the child any harm. Up there you can have no idea how beautiful it is - such fields of gold, such wonderful gardens, such flowers and fruits: it is from there that all the beauty and wealth of the world must come. See all that he has brought with him! and it is all your doing, because you cut the cord of the kite. Oh, clever Bimsha!"

As soon as Bimsha heard that, she ran and got a big kite, and fastening her own child into the strings, started it to fly. "Do not think," cried the envious woman, "that you are the only one whose child is to be clothed in gold! My child is as good as yours any day;wait, and you shall see!"

So presently, when the kite was well up into the clouds, as Katipah's kite had been, she cut the cord, thinking surely that the same fortune would be for her as had been for Katipah. But instead of that, all at once the kite fell headlong to earth, child and all; and when she ran to pick him up, Bimsha found that her son's life had fallen forfeit to her own enviousness and folly.

The wicked woman went green and purple with jealousy and rage; and running to the chief magistrate, she told him that while she was flying a kite with her child fastened to its back, Katipah had come and had cut the string, so that by her doing the child was now dead.

When the magistrate heard that, he sent and caused Katipah to be thrown into prison, and told her that the next day she should certainly be put to death.

Katipah went meekly, carrying her little son in one hand and her blue-and-green kite in the other, for that had become so dear to her she could not now part from it. And all the way to prison Bimsha followed, mocking her, and asking, "Tell us, Katipah, where is your fine husband now?"

In the night the West Wind came and tapped at the prison window, and called tenderly, "Katipah, Katipah, are you there?" And when Katipah got up from her bed of straw and looked out, there was Gamma-gata once more, the beautiful youth whom she loved and had been wedded to, and had heard but had not seen since.

Gamma-gata reached his hands through the bars and put them round her face. "Katipah," he said, "you have become brave: you are fit now to become the wife of the West Wind. To-morrow you shall travel with me all over the world; you shall not stay in one land any more. Now give me our son; for a little while I must take him from you. To prove your courage you must find your own way out of this trouble which you have got into through making a fool of Bimsha."

So Katipah gave him the child through the bars of her prison window, and when he was gone lay down and slept till it became light.

In the morning the chief magistrate and Bimsha, together with the whole populace, came to Katipah's cell to see her led out to death. And when it was found that her child had disappeared, "She is a witch!" they cried; "she has eaten it!" And the chief magistrate said that, being a witch, instead of hanging she was to be burned.

"I have not eaten my child, and I am no witch," said Katipah, as, taking with her her blue-and-green kite she trotted out to the place of execution. When she was come to the appointed spot she said to the chief magistrate, "To every criminal it is permitted to plead in defence of himself; but because I am innocent, am I not also allowed to plead?" The magistrate told her she might speak if she had anything to say.

"All I ask," said Katipah, "is that I may be allowed once more to fly my blue-and-green kite as I used to do in the days when I was happy; and I will show you soon that I am not guilty of what is laid to my charge. It is a very little thing that I ask."

So the magistrate gave her leave; and there before all the people she sent up her kite till it flew high over the roofs of the town. Gently the West Wind took it and blew it away towards the sea. "Oh, Gamma-gata," she whispered softly, "hear me now, for I am not afraid."

The wind blew hard upon the kite, and pulled as though to catch it away, so Katipah twisted the cord once or twice round her waist that she might keep the safer hold over it. Then she said to the chief magistrate and to all the people that were assembled: "I am innocent of all that is charged against me; for, first, it was that wicked Bimsha herself who killed her own child."

"Prove it!" cried the magistrate.

"I cannot," replied Katipah.

"Then you must die!" said the magistrate.

"In the second place," went on Katipah, "I did not eat my own child."

"Prove it!" cried the chief magistrate again.

"I will," said Katipah; "O Gamma-gata, it is a very little thing that I ask."

Down the string of the kite, first a mere speck against the sky, then larger till plain for all to see came the missing one, slithering and sliding, with his golden coat, and the little silver wings tied to his ankles, and handfuls of flowers which he threw into his mother's face as he came. "Oh! cruel chief magistrate," cried Katipah, receiving the babe in her arms, "does it seem that I have eaten him?"

"You are a witch!" said the chief magistrate, "or how do you come to have a child that disappears and comes again from nowhere! It is not possible to permit such things to be: you and your child shall both be burned together!"

Katipah drew softly upon the kite-string. "Oh, Gamma-gata," she cried, "lift me up now very high, and I will not be afraid!"

Then suddenly, before all eyes, Katipah was lifted up by the cord of the kite which she had wound about her waist; right up from the earth she was lifted till her feet rested above the heads of the people.

Katipah, with her babe in her arms, swung softly through the air, out of reach of the hands stretched up to catch her, and addressed the populace in these words:

"Oh, cruel people, who will not believe innocence when it speaks, you must believe me now! I am the wife of the West Wind - of Gamma-gata, the beautiful, the bearer of fine weather, who also brings back the wings that fly till the winter is over. Is it well, do you think, to be at war with the West Wind?

"Ah, foolish ones, I go now, for Gamma-gata calls me, and I am no longer afraid: I go to travel in many lands, whither he carries me, and it will be long before I return here. Many dark days are coming to you, when you shall not feel the west wind, the bearer of fine weather, blowing over you from land to sea; nor shall you see the blossoms open white over the hills, nor feel the earth grow warm as the summer comes in, because the bringer of fair weather is angry with you for the foolishness which you have done. But when at last the west wind returns to you, remember that Katipah, the poor and unprofitable one, is Gamma-gata's wife, and that she has remembered, and has prayed for you."

And so saying, Katipah threw open her arms and let go the cord of the kite which held her safe. "Oh, Gamma-gata," she cried, "I do not see your eyes, but I am not afraid!" And at that, even while she seemed upon the point of falling to destruction, there flashed into sight a fair youth with dark hair and garments full of a storm of flying petals, who, catching up Katipah and her child in his arms, laughed scorn upon those below, and roaring over the roofs of the town, vanished away seawards.

When a chief magistrate and his people, after flagrant wrong-doing, become thoroughly cowed and frightened, they are apt also to be cruel. Poor Bimsha!

Laurence Housman

A CAPFUL OF MOONSHINE

On the top of Drundle Head, away to the right side, where the track crossed, it was known that the fairies still came and danced by night. But though Toonie went that way every evening on his road home from work, never once had he been able to spy them.

So one day he said to the old faggot-maker, "How is it that one gets to see a fairy?" The old man answered, "There are some to whom it comes by nature; but for others three things are needed - a handful of courage, a mouthful of silence, and a capful of moonshine. But if you would be trying it, take care that you don't go wrong more than twice; for with the third time you will fall into the hands of the fairies and be their bondsman. But if you manage to see the fairies, you may ask whatever you like of them."

Toonie believed in himself so much that the very next night he took his courage in both hands, filled his cap with moon-shine, shut his mouth, and set out. Just after he had started he passed, as he thought, a priest riding by on a mule. "Good evening to you, Toonie," called the priest.

"Good evening, your reverence," cried Toonie, and flourished off his cap, so that out fell his capful of moonshine. And though he went on all the way up over the top of Drundle Head, never a fairy did he spy; for he forgot that, in passing what he supposed to be the priest, he had let go both his mouthful of silence and his capful of moonshine.

The next night, when he was coming to the ascent of the hill, he saw a little elderly man wandering uncertainly over the ground ahead of him; and he too seemed to have his hands full of courage and his cap full of moonshine. As Toonie drew near, the other turned about and said to him, "Can you tell me, neighbour, if this be the way to the fairies?"

"Why, you fool," cried Toonie, "a moment ago it was! But now you have gone and let go your mouthful of silence!"

"To be sure, to be sure - so I have!" answered the old man sadly; and turning about, he disappeared among the bushes.

As for Toonie, he went on right over the top of Drundle Head, keeping his eyes well to the right; but never a fairy did he see. For he too had on the way let go his mouthful of silence.

Toonie, when his second failure came home to him, was quite vexed with himself for his folly and misma-nagement. So that it should not happen again, he got his wife to tie on his cap of moonshine so firmly that it could not come off, and to gag up his mouth so that no word could come out of it. And once more taking his courage in both hands, he set out.

For a long way he went and nothing happened, so he was in good hopes of getting the desire of his eyes

Laurence Housman

before the night was over; and, clenching his fists tight upon his courage, he pressed on.

He had nearly reached to the top of Drundle Head, when up from the ground sprang the same little elderly man of the evening before, and began beating him across the face with a hazel wand. And at that Toonie threw up both hands and let go his courage, and turned and tried to run down the hill.

When her husband did not return, Toonie's wife became a kind of a widow. People were very kind to her, and told her that Toonie was not dead - that he had only fallen into the hands of thegood-folk; but all day long she sat and cried, "I fastened on his cap of moonshine, and I tied up his tongue; and for all that he has gone away and left me!" And so she cried until her child was born and named Little Toonie in memory of his lost father.

After a while people, looking at him, began to shake their heads; for as he grew older it became apparent that his tongue was tied, seeing that he remained quite dumb in spite of all that was done to teach him; and his head was full of moonshine, so that he could under-stand nothing clearly by day - only as night came on his wits gathered, and he seemed to find a meaning for things. And some said it was his mother's fault, and some that it was his father's, and some that he was a changeling sent by the fairies, and that the real child had been taken to share his father's bondage. But which of these things was true Little Toonie himself had no idea.

After a time Little Toonie began to grow big, as is the way with children, and at last he became bigger than ever old Toonie had been. But folk still called him Little Toonie, because his head was so full of moonshine; and his mother, finding he was no good to her, sold him to the farmer, by whom, since he had no wits for anything better, he was set to pull at waggon and plough just as if he were a cart-horse; and, indeed, he was almost as strong as one. To make him work, carter and ploughman used to crack their whips over his back; and Little Toonie took it as the most natural thing in the world, because his brain was full of moonshine, so that he understood nothing clearly by day.

But at night he would lie in his stable among the horses, and wonder about the moonlight that stretched wide over all the world and lay free on the bare tops of the hills; and he thought - would it not be good to be there all alone, with the moonbeams laying their white hands down on his head? And so it came that one night, finding the door of his stable unlocked, he ran out into the open world a free man.

A soft wind breathed at large, and swung slowly in the black-silver treetops. Over them Little Toonie could see the quiet slopes of Drundle Head, asleep in the moonlight.

Before long, following the lead of his eyes, he had come to the bottom of the ascent. There before him went walking a little shrivelled elderly man, looking to right and left as if uncertain of the road.

As Little Toonie drew near, the other one turned and spoke. "Can you tell me," said he, "if this be the way to the fairies?"

Little Toonie had no tongue to give an answer; so, looking at his questioner, he wagged his head and went on.

Quickening his pace, the old man came alongside and began peering; then he smiled to himself, and after a bit spoke out. "So you have lost your cap, neighbour? Then you will never be able to find the fairies." For he did not know that Little Toonie, who wore no cap on his head, carried his capful of moonshine safe underneath his skull, where it had been since the hour of his birth.

The little elderly man slipped from his side, disappearing suddenly among the bushes, and Toonie went on alone. So presently he was more than halfway up the ascent, and could see along the foot-track of the thicket the silver moonlight lying out over the open ahead.

He had nearly reached to the top of the hill, when up from the ground sprang the little elderly man, and began beating him across the face with a hazel wand. Toonie thought surely this must be some carter or ploughman beating him to make him go faster; so he made haste to get on and be rid of the blows.

Then, all of a sudden, the little elderly man threw away his hazel stick, and fell down, clutching at Little Toonie's ankles, whining and praying him not to go on.

"Now that I have failed to keep you from coming," he cried, "my masters will put me to death for it! I am a dead man, I tell you, if you go another step!"

Toonie could not understand what the old fellow

meant, and he could not speak to him. But the poor creature clung to his feet, holding them to prevent him from taking another step; so Toonie just stooped down, and (for he was so little and light) picked him up by the scruff, and carried him by his waistband, so that his arms and legs trailed together along the ground.

In the open moonlight ahead little people were all agog; bright dewdrops were shivering down like rain, where flying feet alighted - shot from bent grass-blades like arrows from a drawn bow. Tight, panting little bodies, of which one could count the ribs, and faces flushed with fiery green blood, sprang everywhere. But at Toonie's coming one cried up shriller than a bat; and at once rippling burrows went this way and that in the long grass, and stillness followed after.

The poor, dangling old man, whom Toonie was still carrying, wriggled and whined miserably, crying, "Come back, masters, for it is no use - this one sees you! He has got past me and all my poor skill to stop him. Set me free, for you see I am too old to keep the door for you any longer!"

Out buzzed the fairies, hot and angry as a swarm of bees. They came and fastened upon the unhappy old man, and began pulling him. "To the ant-hills!" they cried; "off with him to the ant-hills!" But when they found that Toonie still held him, quickly they all let go.

One fairy, standing out from the rest, pulled off his cap and bowed low. "What is your will, master mortal?" he inquired; "for until you have taken your wish and gone, we are all slaves at your bidding."

They all cringed round him, the cruel little people; but

Laurence Housman

he answered nothing. The moonbeams came thick, laying their slender white palms graciously upon Toonie's head; and he, looking up, opened his mouth for a laugh that gave no sound.

"Ah, so! That is why - he is a mute!" cried the fairies.

Quickly one dipped his cap along the grass and brought it filled with dew. He sprang up, and poured it upon Toonie's tongue; and as the fairy dew touched it, "Now speak!" they all cried in chorus, and fawned and cringed, waiting for him to give them the word.

Cudgelling his brain for what it all meant, he said, "Tell me first what wish I may have."

"Whatever you like to ask," said they, "for you have become one of our free men. Tell us your name?"

"I am called Little Toonie," said he, "the son of old Toonie that was lost."

"Why, as I live and remember," cried the little elderly man, "old Toonie was me!" Then he threw himself grovelling at his son's feet, and began crying: "Oh, be quick and take me away! Make them give me up to you: ask to have me! I am your poor, loving old father whom you never saw; all these years have I been looking and longing for you! Now take me away, for they are a proud, cruel people, as spiteful as they are small; and my back has been broken twenty years in their bondage."

The fairies began to look blue, for they hate nothing so much as to give up one whom they have once held captive. "We can give you gold," said they, "or precious stones, or the root of long living, or the waters of happiness, or the sap of youth, or the seed of plenty, or the blossom of beauty. Choose any of these, and we can give it you."

The old man again caught hold of his son's feet. "Don't choose these," he whimpered, "choose me!"

So because he had a capful of moonshine in his head, and because the moonbeams were laying their white hands on his hair, he chose the weak, shrivelled old man, who crouched and clung to him, imploring not to be let go.

The fairies, for spite and anger, bestowed every one a parting pinch on their tumble-down old bondsman; then they handed him to his son, and swung back with careless light hearts to their revels.

As father and son went down the hill together, the old man whistled and piped like a bird. "Why, why!" he said, "you are a lad of strength and inches: with you to work and look after me, I can keep on to a merry old age! Ay, ay, I have had long to wait for it; but wisdom is justified in her children."

THE MOON-STROKE

In the hollow heart of an old tree a Jackdaw and his wife had made themselves a nest. As soon as the mother of his eggs had finished laying, she sat waiting patiently for something to come of it. One by one five mouths poked out of the shells, demanding to be fed; so for weeks the happy couple had to be continually in two places at once searching for food to satisfy them.

Presently the wings of the young ones grew strong; they could begin to fly about; and the parents found time for a return to pleasuring and curiosity-hunting. They began gathering in a wise assortment of broken glass and chips of platter to grace the corners of their dwelling. All but the youngest Jackdaw were enchanted with their unutterable beauty and value; they were never tired of quarrelling over the possession and arrangement of them.

"But what are they for?" asked the youngest, a perverse bird who grouped himself apart from the rest, and took no share in their daily squabblings.

The mother-bird said: "They are beautiful, and what God intended for us: therefore they must be true. We may not see the use of them yet, but no doubt some day they will come true."

The little Jackdaw said: "Their corners scratch me when I want to go to sleep; they are far worse than crumbs in the bed. All the other birds do without them - why should not we?"

"That is what distinguishes us from the other birds!" replied the Janedaw, and thanked her stars that it was so.

"I wish we could sing!" sighed the littlest young Jackdaw. "Babble, babble!" replied his mother angrily.

And then, as it was dinner-time, he forgot his grief as they all said grace, and fell-to.

One evening the old Jackdaw came home very late, carrying something that burned bright and green, like an evening star; all the nest shone where he set it down.

"What do you think of that for a discovery?" he said to the Janedaw.

"Think?" she said; "I can't. Some of it looks good to eat; but that fire-patch at the end would burn one's inside out."

Presently the Jackdaw family settled itself down to sleep; only the youngest one sat up and watched. Now he had seen something beautiful. Was it going to come true? Its light was like the song of the nightingale in the leaves overhead: it glowed, and throbbed, and grew strong, flooding the whole place where it lay.

Soon, in the silence, he heard a little wail of grief: "Why have they carried me away here," sighed the

Laurence Housman

glow-worm, "out of the tender grass that loves the ground?"

The littlest Jackdaw listened with all his heart. Now something at last was going to become true, without scratching his legs and making him feel as though crumbs were in his bed.

A little winged thing came flying down to the green light, and two voices began crying together - the glow-worm and its mate.

"They have carried you away?"

"They have carried me away; up here I shall die!"

"I am too weak to lift you," said the one with wings; "you will stay here, and you will die!" Then they cried yet more.

"It seems to me," thought the Jackdaw, "that as soon as the beautiful becomes true, God does not intend it to be for us." He got up softly from among his brothers. "I will carry you down," he said. And without more ado, he picked it up and carried it down out of the nest, and laid it in the long grass at the foot of the tree.

Overhead the nightingale sang, and the full moon shone; its rays struck down on the little Jackdaw's head. For a bird that is not a nightingale to wake up and find its head unprotected under the rays of a full moon is serious: there and then he became moon-struck. He went back into bed; but he was no longer the same little Jackdaw. "Oh, I wish I could sing!" he thought; and not for hours could he get to sleep.

In the morning, when the family woke up, the beautiful and the true was gone. The father Jackdaw thought he nmst have swallowed it in his sleep.

"If you did," said his wife "there'll be a smell of burnt feathers before long!"

But the littlest Jackdaw said, "It came true, and went away, because it was never intended for us."

Now some days after this the old Jack-daw again came carrying something that shone like an evening star - a little spike of gold with a burning emerald set in the end of it. "And what do you think of that?" said he to his wife.

"I daren't come near it," she answered, "for fear it should burn me!"

That night the little Jackdaw lay awake, while all the others slept, waiting to hear the green stone break out into sorrow, and to see if its winged mate would come seeking it. But after hours had gone, and nothing stirred or spoke, he slipped softly out of the nest, and went down to search for the poor little winged mate who must surely be about somewhere.

And now, truly, among the grasses and flowers he heard something sobbing and sighing; a little winged thing darted into sight and out again, searching the ground like a dragon-fly at quest. And all the time, amid the darting and humming of its wings, came sobbing and wringing of hands.

The young Jackdaw called: "Little wings, what have you lost? Is it not a spike with a green light at the

Laurence Housman

end of it?"

"My wand, my wand!" cried the fairy, beside herself with grief. "Just about sunset I was asleep in an empty wren's nest, and when I woke up my wand was gone!"

Then the little Jackdaw, being moon-struck, and not knowing the value of things, flew up to the nest and brought back the fairy her wand.

"Oh!" she cried, "you have saved my life!" And she thanked the Jackdaw till he grew quite modest and shy.

"What is it for? What can you do with it?" he asked.

"With this," she answered, "I can make anything beautiful come true! I can give you whatever you ask; you have but to ask, and you shall have."

Then the little Jackdaw, being moon-struck, and not knowing the value of things, said, "Oh, if I could only sing like a nightingale!"

"You can!" said the fairy, waving her wand but once; and immediately some-thing like a melodious sneeze flew into his head and set it shaking.

"Chiou! chiou! True-true-true-true! Jug! jug! Oh, beautiful! beautiful!" His beak went dabbling in the sweet sound, rippling it this way and that, spraying it abroad out of his blissful heart as a jewel throws out its fires.

The fairy was gone; but the little Jackdaw sprang up into the high elm, and sang on endlessly through the whole night.

At dawn he stopped, and looking down, there he saw the family getting ready for breakfast, and wondering what had become of him. Just as they were saying grace he flew in, his little heart beating with joy over his new-found treasure. What a jewel of a voice he had: better than all the pieces of glass and chips of platter lying down there in the nest! As soon as the parent-birds had finished grace, he lifted his voice and thanked God that the thing he had wished for had become true.

None of them understood what he said, but they paid him plenty of attention. All his brothers and sisters put up their heads and giggled, as the young do when one of their number misbehaves.

"Don't make that noise!" said his mother; "it's not decent!"

"It's low!" said the father-bird.

The littlest young Jackdaw was overwhelmed with astonishment. When he tried to explain, his unseemly melodies led to his immediate expulsion from the family circle. Such noises, he was told, could only be made in private; when he had quite got over them he might come back, - but not until.

He never got over them; so he never came back. For a few days he hid himself in different trees of the garden, and sang the praises of sorrow; but his family, though they comprehended him not, recognised his note, and came searching him with beak and claw, and drove him out so as not to have him near them committing such scandalous noises to the ears of the public.

Laurence Housman

"He lies in his throat!" said the old Jackdaw. "Everything he says he garbles. If he is our son he must have been hatched on the wrong side of the nest!"

After that, wherever he went, all the birds jeered at and persecuted him. Even the nightingales would not listen to his brotherly voice. They made fun of his black coat, and called him a Nonconformist without a conscience. "All this has come about," thought he, "because God never meant anything beautiful to come true."

One day a man who saw him and heard him singing, caught him, and took him round the world in a cage for show. The value of him was discovered. Great crowds came to see the little Jackdaw, and to hear him sing. He was described now as the "Amphabulous Philomel, or the Mongrel-Minstrel"; but it gave him no joy.

Before long he had become what we call tame - that is to say, his wings had been clipped; he was allowed out of his cage, because he could no longer fly away, and he sang when he was told, because he was whipped if he did not.

One day there was a great crowd round the travelling booth where he was on view: the showman had a new wonder which he was about to show to the people. He took the little Jackdaw out of his cage, and set him to perch upon his shoulder, while he busied himself over something which he was taking carefully out of ever so many boxes and coverings. The Jackdaw's sad eye became attracted by a splendid scarf-pin that the showman wore - a gold pin set with a tiny emerald that burned like fire. The bird thought, "Now if only the beautiful could become true!"

And now the showman began holding up a small glass bottle for the crowd to stare into. The people were pushing this way and that to see what might be there.

At the bottom sat the little fairy, without her wand, weeping and beating her hands on the glass.

The showman was so proud he grew red in the face, and ran shouting up and down the plank, shaking and turning the bottle upside down now and then, so as to make the cabined fairy use her wings, and buzz like a fly against the glass.

The Jackdaw waggled unsteadily at his perch on the man's shoulder. "Look at him!" laughed some one in the crowd, "he's going to steal his master's scarf-pin."

"Ho, ho, ho!" shouted the showman. "See this bird now! See the marvelous mongrel nature of the beast! Who tells me he's only a nightingale painted black?"

The people laughed the more at that, for there was a fellow in the crowd looking sheepish. The Jackdaw had drawn out the scarf-pin, and held it gravely in its beak, looking sideways with cunning eyes. He was wishing hard. All the crowd laughed again.

Suddenly the showman's hand gave a jerk, the bottle slipped from his hold and fell, shivering itself upon the ground.

There was a buzz of wings - the fairy had escaped.

"The beautiful is coming true," thought the Jackdaw, as he yielded to the fairy her wand, and found, suddenly, that his wings were not clipped after all.

　　　　　Laurence Housman

"What more can I do for you?" asked the fairy, as they flew away together. "You gave me back my wand; I have given you back your wings."

"I will not ask anything," said the little Jackdaw; "what God intends will come true."

"Let me take you up to the moon," said the fairy. "All the Jackdaws up there sing like nightingales."

"Why is that?" asked the little Jackdaw.

" Because they are all moon-struck," she answered.

"And what is it to be moon-struck?" he asked.

"Surely you should know, if any one!" laughed the fairy. "To see things beautifully, and not as they are. On the moon you will be able to do that without any difficulty."

"Ah," said the little Jackdaw, "now I know at last that the beautiful is going to come true!"

HOW LITTLE DUKE JARL SAVED THE CASTLE

Duke Jarl had found a good roost for himself when his long work of expelling the invader was ended. Seawards and below the town, in the mouth of the river, stood a rock, thrusting out like a great tusk ready to rip up any armed vessel that sought passage that way. On the top of this he had built himself a castle, and its roots went deep, deep down into the solid stone. No man knew how deep the deepest of the foundations went; but wherever they were, just there was old Duke Jarl's sleeping-chamber. Thither he had gone to sleep when the world no longer needed him; and he had not yet returned.

That was three hundred years ago, and still the solid rock vaulted the old warrior's slumber; and over his head men talked of him, and told how he was reserving the strength of his old age till his country should again call for him.

The call seemed to come now; for his descendant, little Duke Jarl the Ninth, was but a child; and being in no fear of him, the old foe had returned, and the castle stood besieged. Also, farther than the eye could see from the topmost tower, the land lay all overrun, its richness laid waste by armed bands who gathered in its harvest by the sword, and the town itself lay under tribute; from the tower one could see the busy quays, and the enemy loading his ships with rich merchandise.

Sent up there to play in safety, little Duke Jarl could not keep his red head from peering over the parapet. He began making fierce faces at the enemy - he was still too young to fight: and quick a grey goose-shaft came and sang its shrill song at his ear. So close had it gone that a little of the ducal blood trickled out over his collar. His face worked with rage; leaning far out over the barrier, he began shouting, "I will tell Duke Jarl of you!" till an attendant ran up and snatched him away from danger.

Things were going badly: the castle was cut off from the land, and on the seaward side the foe had built themselves a great mole within which their war-ships could ride at anchor safe from the reach of storm. Thus there was no way left by which help or provender could come in.

Little Duke Jarl saw men round him growing more gaunt and thin day by day, but he did not understand why till he chanced once upon a soldier gnawing a foul bone for the stray bits of meat that clung to it; then he learned that all in the castle except himself had been put upon quarter-rations, though every day there was more and more fighting work to be done.

So that day when the usual white bread and savouries were brought to him, he flung them all downstairs, telling the cook that the day he really became Duke he would have his head off if he ever dared to send him anything again but the common fare.

Hearing of it, the old Chief Constable picked up little Master Ninth Duke between finger and thumb, and laughed, holding him in the air. "With you alive," said he, "we shall not have to wake Duke Jarl after all!" The little Duke asked when he would let him have a sword; and the Constable clapped his cheeks and ran back cheerfully at a call from the palisades.

But others carried heavy looks, thinking, "Long before his fair promise can come to anything our larders will be empty and our walls gone!"

It was no great time after this that the Duke's Constable was the only man who saw reason in holding out. That became known all through the castle, and the cook, honest fellow, brought up little Jarl's dinner one day with tears in his eyes. He set down his load of dainties. "It is no use!" said he, "you may as well eat to-day, since to-morrow we give up the castle."

"Who dares to say 'we'?" cried little Duke Jarl, springing to his feet.

"All but the Constable," said the cook; "even now they are in the council-hall, trying to make him see reason. Whether or no, they will not let him hold on."

Little Jarl found the doors of the great hall barred to the thunderings of his small fist: for, in truth, these men could not bear to look upon one who had in his veins the blood of old Duke Jarl, when they were about to give up his stronghold to the enemy.

So little Jarl made his way up to the bowery, where was a minstrel's window looking down into the hall. Sticking out his head so that he might see down to where the council was sitting, "If you give up the castle, I will tell Duke Jarl!" he cried. Hearing his

Laurence Housman

young master's voice, the Constable raised his eyes; but not able to see him for tears in them, called out: "Tell him quick, for here it is all against one! Only for one day more have they promised to follow my bidding, and keep the carrion crows from coming to Jarl's nest."

And even as he spoke came the renewed cry of attack, and the answering shout of" Jarl, Jarl!" from the defenders upon the walls. Then all leapt up, over-turning the council-board, and ran out to the battle-ments to carry on with what courage was left to them a hopeless contest for one more day.

Little Duke Jarl remained like a beating heart in the great empty keep. He ran wildly from room to room, calling in rage and desperation on Old Jarl to return and fight. From roof to basement he ran, commanding the spirit of his ancestor to appear, till at last he found himself in the deepest cellars of all. Down there he could hear but faintly the sound of the fighting; yet it seemed to him that through the stone he could hear the slow booming of the sea, and as he went deeper into the castle's foundations the louder had grown its note. "Does the sea come in all the way under the castle?" he wondered. "Oh that it would sap the foundations and sink castle and all, rather than let them give up old Jarl's stronghold to his enemies!"

All was quite dark here, where the castle stood embedded; but now and then little Duke Jarl could feel a puff of wind on his face, and presently he was noticing how it came, as if timed to the booming of the sea underneath: whenever came the sound of a breaking wave, with it came a draught of air. He wondered if, so low down, there might not be some secret opening to the shore.

Groping in the direction of the gusts, his feet came upon stairs. So low and narrow was the entrance, he had to turn sideways and stoop; but when he had burrowed through a thickness of wall he was able to stand upright; and again he found stairs leading somewhere.

Down, these led down. He had never been so low before. And what a storm there must be outside! Against these walls the thunders of: the sea grew so loud he could no longer hear the tramp of his own feet descending.

And now the wind came at him in great gusts; first came the great boom of the sea, and then a blast of air. The way twisted and circled, making his head giddy for a fall; his feet slipped on the steepness and slime of the descent, and at each turn the sound grew more appalling, and the driving force of the wind more and more like the stroke of a man's fist.

Presently the shock of it threw him from his standing, so that he had to lie down and slide feet foremost, clinging with his eyelids and nails to break the violence of his descent. And now the air was so full of thunder that his teeth shook in their sockets, and his bones jarred in his flesh. The darkness growled and roared;the wind kept lifting him backwards - the force of it seemed almost to flay the skin off: his face; and still he went on, throwing his full weight against the air ahead.

Then for a moment he felt himself letting go altogether: solid walls slipping harshly past him in the

Laurence Housman

darkness, he fell; and came headlong, crashed and bruised, to a standstill.

At first his brain was all in a mist; then, raising himself, he saw a dim blue light falling through a low vaulted chamber. At the end of it sat old Jarl, like adamant in slumber. His head was down on his breast, buried in a great burning bush of hair and beard; his hands, gripping the arms of his iron throne, had twisted them like wire; and the weight of his feet where they rested had hollowed a socket in the stone floor for them to sink into.

All his hair and his armour shone with a red-and-blue flame; and the light of him struck the vaulting and the floor like the rays of a torch as it burns. Over his head a dark tunnel, bored in the solid rock, reached up a hollow throat seawards. But not by that way came the wind and the sound of the sea; it was old Jarl himself, breathing peacefully in his sleep, waiting for the hour which should call his strength to life.

Young Duke Jarl ran swiftly across the chamber, and struck old Jarl's knees, crying, "Wake, Jarl! or the castle will be taken!" But the sleeper did not stir. Then he climbed the iron bars of the Duke's chair, and reaching high, caught hold of the red beard. "Forefather!" he cried, "wake, or the castle will be betrayed!"

But still old Duke Jarl snored a drowsy hurricane. Then little Jarl sprang upon his knee, and seizing him by the head, pulled to move its dead weight, and finding he could not, struck him full on the mouth, crying, "Jarl, Jarl, old thunderbolt! wake, or you will betray the castle!"

At that old Jarl hitched himself in his seat, and "Humph!" cried he, drawing in a deep breath.

In rushed the wind whistling from the sea, and down it rushed whistling from the way by which little Jarl had come; like the wings of cranes flying homewards in spring, so it whistled when old Jarl drew in his breath.

Off his knee dropped little Ninth Jarl, buffeted speechless to earth. And old Jarl, letting go one breath, settled himself back to slumber.

Far up overhead, at the darkening-in of night, the besiegers saw the eyes of the castle flash red for an instant, and shut again; then they heard the castle-rock bray out like a great trumpet, and they trembled, crying, "That is old Jarl's warhorn; he is awake out of slumber!"

They had reason enough to fear; for suddenly upon their ships-of-war there crashed, as though out of the bowels of the earth, a black wind and sandblast; and coming, it took the reefed sails and rigging, and snapped the masts and broke every vessel from its moorings, and drove all to wreck and ruin against the great mole that had bccn built to shelter them.

And away inland, beyond the palisades and under the entrenched camp of the besiegers, the ground pitched and rocked, so that every tent fell grovelling; and whenever the ground gaped, captains and men-at-arms were swallowed down in detachments.

Hardly had the call of old Jarl's war-horn ceased, before the Constable commanded the castle gates to be thrown open, and out he came leading a gaunt and hungry band of Jarl-folk warriors; for over in the enemy's camp they had scent of a hot supper which must be cooked and eaten before dawn. And in a little while, when the cooking was at its height, young Duke Jarl stuck his red head out over the battlements, and laughed.

So this has told how old Duke Jarl once turned and talked in his sleep; but to tell of the real awakening of old Jarl would be quite another story.

THE WHITE DOE

One day, as the king's huntsman was riding in the forest, he came to a small pool. Fallen leaves covering its surface had given it the colour of blood, and knee-deep in their midst stood a milk-white doe drinking.

The beauty of the doe set fire to the huntsman's soul; he took an arrow and aimed well at the wild heart of the creature. But as he was loosing the string the branch of a tree overhanging the pool struck him across the face, and caught hold of him by the hair; and arrow and doe vanished away together into the depths of the forest.

Never until now, since he entered the king's service, had the huntsman missed his aim. The thought of the white doe living after he had willed its death inflamed him with rage; he could not rest till he had brought hounds on the trail, determined to follow until it had surrendered to him its life.

All day, while he hunted, the woods stayed breathless, as if to watch; not a blade moved, not a leaf fell. About noon a red deer crossed his path; but he paid no heed, keeping his hounds only to the white doe's trail.

At sunset a fallow deer came to disturb the scent, and through the twilight, as it deepened, a grey wolf ran in

Laurence Housman

and out of the underwood. When night came down, his hounds fled from his call, following through tangled thickets a huge black boar with crescent tusks. So he found himself alone, with his horse so weary that it could scarcely move.

But still, though the moon was slow in its rising, the fever of the chase burned in the huntsman's veins, and caused him to press on. For now he found himself at the rocky entrance of a ravine whence no way led; and the white doe being still before him, he made sure that he would get her at last. So when his horse fell, too tired to rise again, he dismounted and forced his way on; and soon he saw before him the white doe, labouring up an ascent of sharp crags, while closer and higher the rocks rose and narrowed on every side. Presently she had leapt high upon a boulder that shook and swayed as her feet rested, and ahead the wall of rocks had joined so that there was nowhere farther that she might go.

Then the huntsman notched an arrow, and drew with full strength, and let it go. Fast and straight it went, and the wind screamed in the red feathers as they flew; but faster the doe overleapt his aim, and, spurning the stone beneath, down the rough-bouldered gully sent it thundering, shivering to fragments as it fell. Scarcely might the huntsman escape death as the great mass swept past: but when the danger was over he looked ahead, and saw plainly, where the stone had once stood, a narrow opening in the rock, and a clear gleam of moonlight beyond.

That way he went, and passing through, came upon a green field, as full of flowers as a garden, duskily shining now, and with dark shadows in all its folds.

Round it in a great circle the rocks made a high wall, so high that along their crest forest-trees as they clung to look over seemed but as low-growing thickets against the sky.

The huntsman's feet stumbled in shadow and trod through thick grass into a quick-flowing streamlet that ran through the narrow way by which he had entered. He threw himself down into its cool bed, and drank till he could drink no more. When he rose he saw, a little way off, a small dwelling-house of rough stone, moss-covered and cosy, with a roof of wattles which had taken root and pushed small shoots and clusters of grey leaves through their weaving. Nature, and not man, seemed there to have been building herself an abode.

Before the doorway ran the stream, a track of white mist showing where it wound over the meadow; and by its edge a beautiful maiden sat, and was washing her milk-white feet and arms in the wrinkling eddies.

To the huntsman she became all at once the most beautiful thing that the world contained; all the spirit of the chase seemed to be in her blood, and each little movement of her feet made his heart jump for joy. "I have looked for you all my life!" thought he, as he halted and gazed, not daring to speak lest the lovely vision should vanish, and the memory of it mock him for ever.

The beautiful maiden looked up from her washing. "Why have you come here?" said she.

The huntsman answered her as he believed to be the truth, "I have come because I love you!"

"No," she said, "you came because you wanted to kill the white doe. If you wish to kill her, it is not likely that you can love me."

"I do not wish to kill the white doe!" cried the huntsman; "I had not seen you when I wished that. If you do not believe that I love you, take my bow and shoot me to the heart; for I will never go away from you now."

At his word she took one of the arrows, looking curiously at the red feathers, and to test the sharp point she pressed it against her breast. "Have a care!" cried the hunter, snatching it back. He drew his breath sharply and stared. "It is strange," he declared; "a moment ago I almost thought that I saw the white doe."

"If you stay here to-night," said the maiden, "about midnight you will see the white doe go by. Take this arrow, and have your bow ready, and watch! And if to-morrow, when I return, the arrow is still unused in your hand, I will believe you when you say that you love me. And you have only to ask, and I will do all that you desire."

Then she gave the huntsman food and drink and a bed of ferns upon which to rest. "Sleep or wake," said she as she parted from him; "if truly you have no wish to kill the white doe, why should you wake? Sleep!"

"I do not wish to kill the white doe," said the huntsman. Yet he could not sleep: the memory of the one wild creature which had escaped him stung his blood. He looked at the arrow which he held ready, and grew thirsty at the sight of it. "If I see, I must shoot!" cried his hunter's heart. "If I see, I must not shoot!" cried his soul, smitten with love for the beautiful maiden, and remembering her word. "Yet, if I see, I know I must shoot - so shall I lose all!" he cried as midnight approached, and the fever of long waiting remained unassuaged.

Then with a sudden will he drew out his hunting-knife, and scored the palms of his two hands so deeply that he could no longer hold his bow or draw the arrow upon the string. "Oh, fair one, I have kept my word to you!" he cried as midnight came. "The bow and the arrow are both ready."

Looking forth from the threshold by which he lay, he saw pale moonlight and mist making a white haze together on the outer air. The white doe ran by, a body of silver; like quicksilver she ran. And the huntsman, the passion to slay rousing his blood, caught up arrow and bow, and tried in vain with his maimed hands to notch the shaft upon the string.

The beautiful creature leapt lightly by, between the curtains of moonbeam and mist; and as she went she sprang this way and that across the narrow streamlet, till the pale shadows hid her altogether from his sight. "Ah! ah!" cried the huntsman, "I would have given all my life to be able to shoot then! I am the most miserable man alive; but to-morrow I will be the happiest. What a thing is love, that it has known how to conquer in me even my hunter's blood!"

In the morning the beautiful maiden returned; she came sadly. "I gave you my word," said she: "here I am. If you have the arrow still with you as it was last night, I will be your wife, because you have done what never huntsman before was able to do - not to shoot at the white doe when it went by."

The huntsman showed her the unused arrow; her beauty made him altogether happy. He caught her in his arms, and kissed her till the sun grew high. Then she brought food and set it before him; and taking his hand, "I am your wife," said she, "and with all my heart my will is to serve you faithfully. Only, if you value your happiness, do not shoot ever at the white doe." Then she saw that there was blood on his hand, and her face grew troubled. She saw how the other hand also was wounded. "How came this?" she asked; "dear husband, you were not so hurt yesterday."

And the huntsman answered, "I did it for fear lest in the night I should fail, and shoot at the white doe when it came."

Hearing that, his wife trembled and grew white. "You have tricked us both," she said, "and have not truly mastered your desire. Now, if you do not promise me on your life and your soul, or whatever is dearer, never to shoot at a white doe, sorrow will surely come of it. Promise me, and you shall certainly be happy!"

So the huntsman promised faithfully, saying, "On your life, which is dearer to me than my own, I give you my word to keep that it shall be so." Then she kissed him, and bound up his wounds with healing herbs; and to look at her all that day, and for many days after, was better to him than all the hunting the king's forests could provide.

For a whole year they lived together in perfect happiness, and two children came to bless their union -

a boy and a girl born at the same hour. When they were but a month old, they could run; and to see them leaping and playing before the door of their home made the huntsman's heart jump for joy. "They are forest-born, and they come of a hunter's blood; that is why they run so early, and have such limbs," said he.

"Yes," answered his wife, "that is partly why. When they grow older they will run so fast - do not mistake them for deer if ever you go hunting."

No sooner had she said the word than the memory of it, which had slept for a whole year, stirred his blood. The scent of the forest blew up through the rocky ravine, which he had never repassed since the day when he entered, and he laid his hands thoughtfully on the weapons he no longer used.

Such restlessness took hold of him all that day that at night he slept ill, and, waking, found himself alone with no wife at his side. Gazing about the room, he saw that the cradle also was empty. "Why," he wondered, "have they gone out together in the middle of the night?"

Yet he gave it little more thought, and turning over, fell into a troubled sleep, and dreamed of hunting and of the white doe that he had seen a year before stooping to drink among the red leaves that covered the forest pool.

In the morning his wife was by his side, and the little ones lay asleep upon their crib. "Where were you," he asked, "last night? I woke, and you were not here."

His wife looked at him tenderly, and sighed. "You

Laurence Housman

should shut your eyes better," said she. "I went out to see the white doe, and the little ones came also. Once a year I see her; it is a thing I must not miss."

The beauty of the white doe was like strong drink to his memory: the beautiful limbs that had leapt so fast and escaped - they alone, of all the wild life in the world, had conquered him. "Ah!" he cried, "let me see her, too; let her come tame to mv hand, and I will not hurt her!"

His wife answered: "The heart of the white doe is too wild a thing; she cannot come tame to the hand of any hunter under heaven. Sleep again, dear husband, and wake well! For a whole year you have been sufficiently happy; the white doe would only wound you again in your two hands."

When his wife was not by, the hunter took the two children upon his knee, and said, "Tell me, what was the white doe like? what did she do? and what way did she go?"

The children sprang off his knee, and leapt to and fro over the stream. "She was like this," they cried, "and she did this, and this was the way she went!" At that the hunter drew his hand over his brow. "Ah," he said, "I seemed then almost to see the white doe."

Little peace had he from that day. Whenever his wife was not there he would call the little ones to him, and cry, "Show me the white doe and what she did." And the children would leap and spring this way and that over the little stream before the door, crying, "She was like this, and she did this, and this was the way she went!"

The huntsman loved his wife and children with a deep affection, yet he began to have a dread that there was something hidden from his eyes which he wished yet feared to know. "Tell me," he cried one day, half in wrath, when the fever of the white doe burned more than ever in his blood, "tell me where the white doe lives, and why she comes, and when next. For this time I must see her, or I shall die of the longing that has hold of me!" Then, when his wife would give no answer, he seized his bow and arrows and rushed out into the forest, which for a whole year had not known him, slaying all the red deer he could find.

Many he slew in his passion, but he brought none of them home, for before the end a strange discovery came to him, and he stood amazed, dropping the haunch which he had cut from his last victim. "It is a whole year," he said to himself, "that I have not tasted meat; I, a hunter, who love only the meat that I kill!"

Returning home late, he found his wife troubling her heart over his long absence. "Where have you been?" she asked him, and the question inflamed him into a fresh passion.

"I have been out hunting for the white doe," he cried; "and she carries a spot in her side where some day my arrow must enter. If I do not find her I shall die!"

His wife looked at him long and sorrowfully; then she said: "On your life and soul be it, and on mine also, that your anger makes me tell what I would have kept hidden. It is to-night that she comes. Now it remains for you to remember your word once given to me!"

"Give it back to me!" he cried; "it is my fate to finish

Laurence Housman

the quest of the white doe."

"If I give it," said she, "your happiness goes with it, and mine, and that of our children."

"Give it back to me!" he said again; "I cannot live unless I may master the white doe! If she will come tame to my hand, no harm shall happen to her."

And when she denied him again, he gave her his bow and arrows, and bade her shoot him to the heart, since without his word rendered back to him he could not live.

Then his wife took both his hands and kissed them tenderly, and with loud weeping quickly set him free of his promise. "As well," said she, "ask the hunter to go bound to the lion's den as the white doe to come tame into your keeping; though she loved you with all her heart, you could not look at her and not be her enemy." She gazed on him with full affection, and sighed deeply. "Lie down for a little," she said, "and rest; it is not till midnight that she comes. When she comes I will wake you."

She took his head in her hands and set it upon her knee, making him lie down. "If she will come and stand tame to my hand," he said again, "then I will do her no harm."

After a while he fell asleep; and, dreaming of the white doe, started awake to find it was already midnight, and the white doe standing there before him. But as soon as his eyes lighted on her they kindled with such fierce ardour that she trembled and sprang away out of the door and across the stream. "Ah, ah, white doe, white doe!" cried the wind in the feathers of the shaft that flew after her.

Just at her leaping of the stream the arrow touched her; and all her body seemed to become a mist that dissolved and floated away, broken into thin fragments over the fast-flowing stream.

By the hunter's side his wife lay dead, with an arrow struck into her heart. The door of the house was shut; it seemed to be only an evil dream from which he had suddenly awakened. But the arrow gave real substance to his hand: when he drew it out a few true drops of blood flowed after. Suddenly the hunter knew all he had done. "Oh, white doe, white doe!" he cried, and fell down with his face to hers.

At the first light of dawn he covered her with dried ferns, that the children might not see how she lay there dead. "Run out," he cried to them, "run out and play! Play as the white doe used to do!" And the children ran out and leapt this way and that across the stream, crying, "She was like this, and she did this, and this was the way she went!"

So while they played along the banks of the stream, the hunter took up his beautiful dead wife and buried her. And to the children he said, "Your mother has gone away; when the white doe comes she will return also."

"She was like this," they cried, laughing and playing, "and she did this, and this was the way she went!" And all the time as they played he seemed to see the white doe leaping before him in the sunlight.

That night the hunter lay sleepless on his bed, wishing

Laurence Housman

for the world to end; but in the crib by his side the two children lay in a sound slumber. Then he saw plainly in the moonlight the white doe, with a red mark in her side, standing still by the doorway. Soon she went to where the young ones were lying, and, as she touched the coverlet softly with her right fore-foot, all at once two young fawns rose up from the ground and sprang away into the open, following where the white doe beckoned them.

Nor did they ever return. For the rest of his life the huntsman stayed where they left him, a sorrowful and lonely man. In the grave where lay the woman's form he had slain he buried his bow and arrows far from the sight of the sun or the reach of his own hand; and coming to the place night by night, he would watch the mists and the moonrise, and cry, "White doe, white doe, will you not some day forgive me?" and did not know that she had forgiven him when, before she died, she kissed his two hands and made him sleep for the last time with his head on her knee.

THE GENTLE COCKATRICE

Far above the terraces of vine, where the goat pastures ended and the rocks began, the eye could take a clear view over the whole plain. From that point the world below spread itself out like a green map, and the only walls one could see were the white flanks and tower of the cathedral rising up from the grey roofs of the city; as for the streets, they seemed to be but narrow foot-tracks, on which people appeared like ants walking.

This was the view of the town which Beppo, the son of the common hangman, loved best. It was little pleasure to him to be down there, where all the other lads drove him from their play: for the hang-man had had too much to do with the fathers and brothers of some of them, and his son was not popular. When there was a hanging they would rush off to the public square to see it; afterwards they made it their sport to play at hanging Beppo, if by chance they could catch him; and that play had a way at times of coming uncomfortably near to reality.

Beppo did not himself go to the square when his father's trade was on; the near view did not please him. Perched on the rocky hillside, he would look down upon a gathering of black specks, where two others stood detached upon a space in their midst, and would know that there his father was hanging a man.

Laurence Housman

Sometimes it was more than one, and that made Beppo afraid. For he knew that for every man that he hanged his father took a dram to give him courage for the work; and if there were several poor fellows to be cast off from life, the hangman was not pleasant company afterwards for those very near and dear to him.

It happened one day that the hangman was to give the rope to five fellows, the most popular and devil-may-care rakes and roysterers in the whole town. Beppo was up very early that morning, and at the first streak of light had dropped himself over the wall into the town ditch, and was away for the open country and the free air of the hills; for he knew that neither at home nor in the streets would life be worth living for a week after, because of all the vengeances that would fall on him.

Therefore he had taken from the home larder a loaf of bread and a clump of dried figs; and with these hoped to stand the siege of a week's solitude rather than fall in with the hard dealings of his own kind. He knew a cave, above where the goats found pasture, out of which a little red, rusty water trickled; there he thought to make himself a castle and dream dreams, and was sure he would be happy enough, if only he did not grow afraid.

Beppo had discovered the cave one day from seeing a goat push out through a thicket of creepers on the side of the hill; and, hidden under their leaves, he had found it a wonderful, cool refuge from the heat of summer noons. Now, as he entered, the place struck very cold; for it was early spring, and the earth was not yet warmed through with the sun. So he set himself to gather dead grass, and briers, and tufts of goat's hair, and from farther down the hillside the wood of a ruined goat-paddock, till he had a great store of fuel at hand. He worked all day like a squirrel for its winter hoard; and as his pile mounted he grew less and less afraid of the cave where he meant to live.

Seeing so large a heap of stuff ready for the feeding of his fire, he began to rise to great heights in his own imagination. First he had been a poor outlaw, a mere sheep-stealer hiding from men's clutches; then he became a robber-chief; and at last he was no less than the king of the mountains.

"This mountain is all caves," he said to himself, "and all the caves are full of gold; and I am the king to whom it all belongs."

In the evening Beppo lighted his fire, in the far back of his cave, where its light would not be seen, and sat down by its warmth to eat dried figs and bread and drink brackish water. To-morrow he meant to catch a kid and roast it and eat it. Why should he ever go home again? Kid was good - he did not get that to eat when he was at home; and now in the streets the boys must be looking for him to play at their cruel game of hanging. Why should he go back at all?

The fire licked its way up the long walls of the cavern; slowly the warmth crept round on all sides. The rock where Beppo laid his hand was no longer damp and cold; he made himself a bed of the driest litter in a niche close to the fire, laid his head on a smooth knob of stone, and slept. But even in his sleep he remembered his fire, dreading to awake and find himself in darkness. Every time the warmth of it diminished he raised himself and put on more fuel.

Laurence Housman

In the morning - for faint blue edges of light marking the ridged throat of the cavern told that outside the day had begun - he woke fully, and the fire still burned. As he lay, his pillow of rock felt warm and almost soft; and, strangely enough, through it there went a beating sound as of blood. This must be his own brain that he heard; but he lifted his head, and where he laid his hand could feel a slow movement of life going on under it. Then he stared hard at the overhanging rock, and surely it heaved softly up and down, like some great thing breathing slowly in its sleep.

Yet he could make out no shape at all till, having run to the other side of the cave, he turned to see the whole face of the rock which seemed to be taking on life. Then he realised very gradually what looked to be the throat and jaws of a great monster lying along the ground, while all the rest passed away into shadow or lay buried under masses of rock, which closed round it like a mould. Below the nether jaw-bone the flames licked and caressed the throat; and the tough, mud-coloured hide ruffled and smoothed again as if grateful for the heat that tickled its way in.

Very slowly indeed the great Cockatrice, which had lain buried for thousands of years, out of reach of the light or heat of the sun, was coming round again to life. That was Beppo's own doing, and for some very curiotls reason he was not afraid.

His heart was uplifted. "This is my cave," thought he, "so this must be my Cockatrice! Now I will ride out on him and conquer the world. I shall be really a king then!"

He guessed that it must have been the warmth which

had waked the Cockatrice, so he made fires all down the side of the cave; wherever the great flank of the Cockatrice seemed to show, there he lighted a fire to put heat into the slumbering body of the beast.

"Warm up, old fellow," he cried; "thaw out, I tell you! I want you to talk to me."

Presently the mouth of the Cockatrice unsealed itself, and began to babble of green fields. "Hay - I want hay!" said the Cockatrice; "or grass. Does the world contain any grass?"

Beppo went out, and presently returned with an armful. Very slowly the Cockatrice began munching the fresh fodder, and Beppo, intent on feeding him back to life, ran to and fro between the hillside and the cavern till he was exhausted and could go no more. He sat down and watched the Cockatrice finish his meal.

Presently, when the monster found that his fodder was at an end, he puckered a great lid, and far up aloft in the wall of the cave flashed out a green eye.

If all the emeralds in the world were gathered together, they might shine like that; if all the glow-worms came up out of the fields and put their tails together, they might make as great an orb of fire. All the cave looked as green as grass when the eye of the Cockatrice lighted on it; and Beppo, seeing so mighty an optic turning its rays on him, felt all at once shrivelled and small, and very weak at the knees.

"Oh, Cockatrice," he said, in a mon-strous sad voice, "I hope I haven't hurt you!"

Laurence Housman

"On the contrary," said the Cockatrice, "you have done me much good. What are you going to do with me now?"

"I do with you?" cried Beppo, astonished at so wild a possibility offering to come true. "I would like to get you out, of course - but can I?"

"I would like that dearly also!" said the Cockatrice.

"But how can I?" inquired Beppo.

"Keep me warm and feed me," re-turned the monster. "Presently I shall be able to find out where my tail is. When I can move that I shall be able to get out."

Beppo undertook whatever the Cockatrice told him - it was so grand to have a Cockatrice of his own. But it was a hard life, stoking up fires day and night, and bringing the Cockatrice the fodder necessary to replenish his drowsy being. When Beppo was quite tired out he would colne and lay his head against the monster's snout; and the Cockatrice would open a benevolent eye and look at him affectionately.

"Dear Cockatrice," said the boy one day, "tell me about yourself, and how you lived and what the world was like when you were free!"

"Do you see any green in my eye?" said the Cockatrice.

"I do, indeed!" said Beppo. "I never saw anything so green in all the world."

"That's all right, then!" said the Cockatrice. "Climb up

and look in, and you will see what the world was like when I was young."

So Beppo climbed and scrambled, and slipped and clung, till he found himself on the margin of a wonderful green lake, which was but the opening into the whole eye of the Cockatrice.

And as soon as Beppo looked, he had lost his heart for ever to the world he saw there. It was there, quite real before him: a whole world full of living and moving things - the world before the trouble of man came to it.

"I see green hills, and fields, and rocks, and trees," cried Beppo, "and among them a lot of little Cockatrices are playing!"

"They were my brothers and sisters; I remember them," said the Cockatrice. "I have them all in my mind's eye. Call them - perhaps they will come and talk to you; you will find them very nice and friendly."

"They are too far off," said Beppo, "they cannot hear me."

"Ah, yes," murmured the Cockatrice, "memory is a wonderful thing!"

When Beppo came down again he was quite giddy, and lost in wonder and joy over the beautiful green world the Cockatrice had shown him. "I like that better than this!" said he.

"So do I," said the Cockatrice. "But perhaps, when my tail gets free, I shall feel better."

Laurence Housman

One morning he said to Beppo: "I do really begin to feel my tail. It is somewhere away down the hill yonder. Go and look out for me, and tell me if you can see it moving."

So Beppo went to the mouth of the cave, and looked out towards the city, over all the rocks and ridges and goat-pastures and slopes of vine that lay between.

Suddenly, as he looked, the steeple of the cathedral tottered, and down fell its weathercock and two of its pinnacles, and half the chimneys of the town snapped off their tops. All that distance away Beppo could hear the terrified screams of the inhabitants as they ran out of their houses in terror.

"I've done it!" cried the Cockatrice, from within the cave.

"But you mustn't do that!" exclaimed Beppo in horror.

"Mustn't do what?" inquired the Cockatrice.

"You mustn't wag your tail! You don't know what you are doing!"

"Oh, master!" wailed the Cockatrice; "mayn't I? For the first time this thousand years I have felt young again."

Beppo was pale and trembling with agitation over the fearful effects of that first tail-wagging. "You mustn't feel young!" said he.

"Why not?" asked the Cockatrice, with a piteous wail.

"There isn't room in the world for a Cockatrice to feel young nowadays," answered Beppo gravely.

"But, dear little master and benefactor," cried the Cockatrice, "what did you wake me up for?"

"I don't know," replied Beppo, terribly perplexed. "I wouldn't have done it had I known where your tail was."

"Where is it?" inquired the Cockatrice, with great interest. "It's right underneath the city where I mean to be king," said Beppo; "and if you move it the city will come down; and then I shall have nothing to be king of."

"Very well," said the Cockatrice sadly; "I will wait!"

"Wait for what?" thought Beppo. "Waiting won't do any good." And he began to think what he must do. "You lie quite still!" said he to the Cockatrice. "Go to sleep, and I will still look after you."

"Oh, little master," said the Cockatrice, "but it is difficult to go to sleep when the delicious trouble of spring is in one's tail! How long does this city of yours mean to stay there? I am so alive that I find it hard to shut an eye!"

"I will let the fires that keep you warm go down for a bit," said Beppo, "and you mustn't eat so much grass; then you will feel better, and your tail will be less of an anxiety."

And presently, when Beppo had let the fires which warmed him get low, and had let time go by without

Laurence Housman

bringing him any fresh fodder, the Cockatrice dozed off into an uneasy, prehistoric slumber.

Then Beppo, weeping bitterly over his treachery to the poor beast which had trusted him, raked open the fires and stamped out the embers; and, leaving the poor Cockatrice to get cold, ran down the hill as fast as he could to the city he had saved - the city of which he meant to be king.

He had been away a good many days, but the boys in the street were still on the watch for him. He told them how he had saved the city from the earth-quake; and they beat him from the city gate to his father's door. He told his own father how he had saved the city; and his father beat him from his own door to the city gate. Nobody believed him.

He lay outside the town walls till it was dark, all smarting with his aches and pains; then, when nobody could see him, he got up and very miserably made his way back to the cave on the hill. And all the way he said to himself, "Shall I put fire under the Cockatrice once more, and make him shake the town into ruins? Would not that be fine?"

Inside, the cave was quite still and cold, and when he laid his hand on the Cockatrice he could not feel any stir or warmth in its bones. Yet when he called, the Cockatrice just opened a slit of his green eye and looked at him with trust and affection.

"Dear Cockatrice," cried Beppo, "forgive me for all the wrong I have done you!" And as he clambered his way toward the green light, a great tear rolled from under the heavy lid and flowed past him like a cataract.

"Dear Cockatrice," cried Beppo again, when he stood on the margin of the green lake, "take me to sleep with you in the land where the Cockatrices are at play, and keep quite still with your tail!"

Slowly and painfully the Cockatrice opened his eye enough to let Beppo slip through; and Beppo saw the green world with its playful cockatrices waiting to welcome him. Then the great eyelid shut down fast, and the waking days of the Cockatrice were over. And Beppo's native town lay safe, because he had learned from the Cockatrice to be patient and gentle, and had gone to be king of a green world where everything was harmless.

Laurence Housman

THE RAT-CATCHER'S DAUGHTER

Once upon a time there lived an old rat-catcher who had a daughter, the most beautiful girl that had ever been born. Their home was a dirty little cabin; but they were not so poor as they seemed, for every night the rat-catcher took the rats he had cleared out of one house and let them go at the door of another, so that on the morrow he might be sure of a fresh job.

His rats got quite to know him, and would run to him when he called; people thought him the most wonderful rat-catcher, and could not make out how it was that a rat remained within reach of his operations.

Now any one can see that a man who practised so cunning a roguery was greedy beyond the intentions of Providence. Every day, as he watched his daughter's beauty increase, his thoughts were: "When will she be able to pay me back for all the expense she has been to me?" He would have grudged her the very food she ate, if it had not been necessary to keep her in the good looks which were some day to bring him his fortune. For he was greedier than any gnome after gold.

Now all good gnomes have this about them: they love whatever is beautiful, and hate to see harm happen to it. A gnome who lived far away underground below where stood the rat-catcher's house, said to his fellows:

"Up yonder is a man who has a daughter; so greedy is he, he would sell her to the first comer who gave him gold enough! I am going up to look after her."

So one night, when the rat-catcher set a trap, the gnome went and got himself caught in it. There in the morning, when the rat-catcher came, he found a funny little fellow, all bright and golden, wriggling and beating to be free.

"I can't get out!" cried the little gnome. "Let me go!"

The rat-catcher screwed up his mouth to look virtuous. "If I let you out, what will you give me?" "A sack full of gold," answered the gnome, "just as heavy as myself - not a pennyweight less!"

"Not enough!" said the rat-catcher. "Guess again!"

"As heavy as you are!" cried the gnome, beginning to plead in a thin, whining tone.

"I'm a poor man," said the rat-catcher; "a poor man mayn't afford to be generous!"

"What is it you want of me?" cried the gnome.

"If I let you go," said the rat-catcher, "you must make me the richest man in the world!" Then he thought of his daughter: "Also you must make the king's son marry my daughter; then I will let you go."

The gnome laughed to himself to see how the trapper was being trapped in his own avarice as, with the most melancholy air, he answered: "I can make you the richest man in the world; but I know of no way of

Laurence Housman

making the king's son marry your daughter, except one."

"What way?" asked the rat-catcher.

"Why," answered the gnome, "for three years your daughter must come and live with me underground, and by the end of the third year her skin will be changed into pure gold like ours. And do you know any king's son who would refuse to marry a beautiful maiden who was pure gold from the sole of her foot to the crown of her head?"

The rat-catcher had so greedy an inside that he could not believe in any king's son refusing to marry a maiden of pure gold. So he clapped hands on the bargain, and let the gnome go.

The gnome went down into the ground, and fetched up sacks and sacks of gold, until he had made the rat-catcher the richest man in the world. Then the father called his daughter, whose name was Jasome', and bade her follow the gnome down into the heart of the earth. It was all in vain that Jasome' begged and implored; the rat-catcher was bent on having her married to the king's son. So he pushed, and the gnome pulled, and down she went; and the earth closed after her.

The gnome brought her down to his home under the hill upon which stood the town. Everywhere round her were gold and precious stones; the very air was full of gold dust, so that when she remained still it settled on her hands and her hair, and a soft golden down began to show itself over her skin. So there in the house of the gnome sat Jasome', and cried; and, far away overhead, she heard the days come and go, by the sound of people walking and the rolling of wheels.

The gnome was very kind to her; nothing did he spare of underground commodities that might afford her pleasure. He taught her the legends of all the heroes that have gone down into earth, and been forgotten, and the lost songs of the old poets, and the buried languages that once gave wisdom to the world: down there all these things are remembered.

She became the most curiously accomplished and wise maiden that ever was hidden from the light of day. "I have to train you," said the gnome, "to be fit for a king's bride!" But Jasome', though she thanked him, only cried to be let out.

In front of the rat-catcher's house rose a little spring of salt water with gold dust in it, that gilded the basin where it sprang. When he saw it, he began rubbing his hands with delight, for he guessed well enough that his daughter's tears had made it; and the dust in it told him how surely now she was being turned into gold.

And now the rat-catcher was the richest man in the world: all his traps were made of gold, and when he went rat-hunting he rode in a gilded coach drawn by twelve hundred of the finest and largest rats. This was for an advertisement of the business. He now caught rats for the fun of it, and the show of it, but also to get money by it; for, though he was so rich, ratting and money-grubbing had become a second nature to him: unless he were at one or the other, he could not be happy.

Far below, in the house of the gnome, Jasome' sat and

cried. When the sound of the great bells ringing for Easter came down to her, the gnome said: "To-day I cannot bind you; it is the great rising day for all Christians. If you wish, you may go up, and ask your father now to release you."

So Jasome' kissed the gnome, and went up the track of her own tears, that brought her to her father's door. When she came to the light of day, she felt quite blind; a soft yellow tint was all over her, and already her hair was quite golden.

The rat-catcher was furious when he saw her coming back before her time. "Oh, father," she cried, "let me come back for a little while to play in the sun!" But her father, fearing lest the gilding of her complexion should be spoiled, drove her back into the earth, and trampled it down over her head.

The gnome seemed quite sorry for her when she returned; but already, he said, a year was gone - and what were three years, when a king's son would be the reward?

At the next Easter he let her go again; and now she looked quite golden, except for her eyes, and her white teeth, and the nails on her pretty little fingers and toes. But again her father drove her back into the ground, and put a heavy stone slab over the spot to make sure of her.

At last the third Easter came, and she was all gold. She kissed the gnome many times, and was almost sorry to leave him, for he had been very kind to her. And now he told her about her father catching him in the trap, and robbing him of his gold by a hard bargain, and of his being forced to take her down to live with him, till she was turned into gold, so that she might marry the king's son. "For now," said he, "you are so compounded of gold that only the gnomes could rub it off you."

So this time, when Jasome' came up once more to the light of day, she did not go back again to her cruel father, but went and sat by the roadside, and played with the sunbeams, and wondered when the king's son would come and marry her. And as she sat there all the country-people who passed by stopped and mocked her; and boys came and threw mud at her because she was all gold from head to foot - an object, to be sure, for all simple folk to laugh at. So presently, instead of hoping, she fell to despair, and sat weeping, with her face hidden in her hands.

Before long the king's son came that road, and saw something shining like sunlight on a pond; but when he came near, he found a lovely maiden of pure gold lying in a pool of her own tears, with her face hidden in her hair.

Now the king's son, unlike the country-folk, knew the value of gold; but he was grieved at heart for a maiden so stained all over with it, and more, when he beheld how she wept. So he went to lift her up; and there, surely, he saw the most beautiful face he could ever have dreamed of. But, alas! So discoloured - even her eyes, and her lips, and the very tears she shed were the colour of gold! When he could bring her to speak, she told him how, because she was all gold, all the people mocked at her, and boys threw mud at her; and she had nowhere to go, unless it were back to the kind gnome who lived underground, out of sight of the sweet sun.

Laurence Housman

So the prince said, "Come with me, and I will take you to my father's palace, and there nobody shall mock you, but you shall sit all your days in the sunshine, and be happy." And as they went, more and more he wondered at her great beauty - so spoiled that he could not look at her without grief - and was taken with increasing wonder at the beautiful wisdom stored in her golden mind; for she told him the tales of the heroes which she had learned from the gnome, and of buried cities; also the songs of old poets that have been forgotten; and her voice, like the rest of her, was golden.

The prince said to himself, "I shut my eyes, and am ready to die loving her; yet, when I open them, she is but a talking statue!"

One day he saki to her, "Under all this disguise you must be the most beautiful thing upon earth! Already to me you are the dearest!" and he sighed, for he knew that a king's son might not marry a figure of gold. Now one day after this, as Jasome' sat alone in the sunshine and cried, the little old gnome stood before her, and said, "Well, Jasome', have you married the king's son?"

"Alas!" cried Jasome', "you have so changed me: I am no longer human! Yet he loves me, and, but for that, he would marry me."

"Dear me!" said the gnome. "If that is all, I can take the gold off you again: why, I said so!"

Jasome' entreated him, by all his former kindness, to do so for her now.

"Yes," said the gnome, "but a bargain is a bargain.

Now is the time for me to get back my bags of gold. Do you go to your father, and let him know that the king's son is willing to marry you if he restores to me my treasure that he took from me; for that is what it comes to."

Up jumped Jasome', and ran to the rat-catcher's house. "Oh, father," she cried, "now you can undo all your cruelty to me; for now, if you will give back the gnome his gold, he will give my own face back to me, and I shall marry the king's son!"

But the rat-catcher was filled with admiration at the sight of her, and would not believe a word she said. "I have given you your dowry," he answered; "three years I had to do without you to get it. Take it away, and get married, and leave me the peace and plenty I have so hardly earned!"

Jasome' went back and told the gnome.

"Really," said he, "I must show this rat-catcher that there are other sorts of traps, and that it isn't only rats and gnomes that get caught in them! I have given him his taste of wealth; now it shall act as pickle to his poverty!"

So the next time the rat-catcher put his foot out of doors the ground gave way under it, and, snap! - the gnome had him by the leg.

"Let me go!" cried the rat-catcher; "I can't get out!"

"Can't you?" said the gnome. "If I let you out, what will you give me?"

"My daughter!" cried the rat-catcher; "my beautiful golden daughter!"

"Oh no! "laughed the gnome. "Guess again!" "My own weight in gold!" cried the rat-catcher, in a frenzy; but the gnome would not close the bargain till he had wrung from the rat-catcher the promise of his last penny.

So the gnome carried away all the sacks of gold before the rat-catcher's eyes; and when he had them safe underground, then at last he let the old man go. Then he called Jasome' to follow him, and she went down willingly into the black earth.

For a whole year the gnome rubbed and scrubbed and tubbed her to get the gold out of her composition; and when it was done, she was the most shiningly beautiful thing you ever set eyes on.

When she got back to the palace, she found her dear prince pining for love of her, and wondering when she would return. So they were married the very next day; and the rat-catcher came to look on at the wedding.

He grumbled because he was in rags, and because he was poor; he wept that he had been robbed of his money and his daughter. But gnomes and daughters, he said, were in one and the same box; such ingratitude as theirs no one could beat

WHITE BIRCH

Once upon a time there lived in a wood a brother and sister who had been forgotten by all the world. But this thing did not greatly grieve their hearts, because they themselves were all the world to each other: meeting or parting, they never forgot that. Nobody remained to tell them who they were; but she was "Little Sister," and he was "Fair Brother," and those were the only names they ever went by.

In their little wattled hut they would have been perfectly happy but for one thing which now and then they remembered and grieved over. Fair Brother was lame - not a foot could he put to the ground, nor take one step into the outside world. But he lay quiet on his bed of leaves, while Little Sister went out and in, bringing him food and drink, and the scent of flowers, and tales of the joy of earth and of the songs of birds.

One day she brought him a litter of withered birch-leaves to soften his bed and make it warmer for the approaching season of cold; and all the winter he lay on it, and sighed. Little Sister had never seen him so sad before.

In the spring, when the songs of the pairing birds began, his sorrow only grew greater. "Let me go out, let me go out," he cried; "only a little way into the

Laurence Housman

bright world before I die!" She kissed his feet, and took him up in her arms and carried him. But she could only go a very little way with her burden; presently she had to return and lay him down again on his bed of leaves.

"Have I seen all the bright world?" he asked. "Is it such a little place?"

To hide her sorrow from him, Little Sister ran out into the woods, and as she went, wondering how to comfort his grief, she could not help weeping.

All at once at the foot of a tree she saw the figure of a woman seated. It was strange, for she had never before seen anybody else in the wood but themselves. The woman said to her, "Why is it that you weep so?"

"The heart of Fair Brother is breaking," replied Little Sister. "It is because of that that I am weeping."

"Why is his heart breaking?" inquired the other. "I do not know," answered Little Sister. "Ever since last autumn fell it has been so. Always, before, he has been happy; he has no reason not to be, only he is lame."

She had come close to the seated figure; and looking, she saw a woman with a very white skin, in a robe and hood of deep grey. Grey eyes looked back at her with just a soft touch in them of the green that comes with the young leaves of spring.

"You are beautiful," said Little Sister, drawing in her breath. "Yes, I am beautiful," answered the other. "Why is Fair Brother lame? Has he no feet?"

"Oh, beautiful feet!" said Little Sister. "But they are like still water; they cannot run."

"If you want him to run," said the other, "I can tell you what to do. What will you give me in exchange?"

"Whatever you like to ask," answered Little Sister; "but I am poor."

"You have beautiful hair," said the woman; "will you let that go?"

Little Sister stooped down her head, and let the other cut off her hair. The wind went out of it with a sigh as it fell into the grey woman's lap. She hid it away under her robe, and said, "Listen, Little Sister, and I will tell you! To-night is the new moon. If you can hold your tongue till the moon is full, the feet of Fair Brother shall run like a stream from the hills, dancing from rock to rock."

"Only tell me what I must do!" said Little Sister.

"You see this birch-tree, with its silver skin?" said the wonmn. "Cut off two strips of it and weave them into shoes for Fair Brother. And when they are finished by the full moon, if you have not spoken, you have but to put them upon Fair Brother's feet, and they will outrun yours."

So Little Sister, as the other had told her, cut off two strips from the bark of the birch-tree, and ran home as fast as she could to tell her brother of the happiness which, with only a little waiting, was in store for them. But as she came near home, over the low roof she saw the new moon hanging like a white feather in the air;

and, closing her lips, she went in and kissed Fair
Brother silently.

He said, "Little Sister, loose out your hair over me, and
let me feel the sweet airs; and tell me how the earth
sounds, for my heart is sick with sorrow and longing."
She took his hand and laid it upon her heart that he
might feel its happy beating, but said no word. Then
she sat down at his feet and began to work at the shoes.
All the birch-bark she cut into long strips fit for
weaving, doing everything as the grey woman had told
her.

Fair Brother fretted at her silence, and cried, calling
her cruel; but she only kissed his feet, and went on
working the faster. And the white birch shoes grew
under her hands; and every night she watched and saw
the moon growing round.

Fair Brother said, "Little Sister, what have you done
with your hair in which you used to fetch home the
wind? And why do you never go and bring me flowers
or sing me the song of the birds?" And Little Sister
looked up and nodded, but never answered or moved
from her task, for her fingers were slow, and the moon
was quick in its growing.

One night Fair Brother was lying asleep, and his head
was filled with dreams of the outer world into which
he longed to go. The full moon looked in through the
open door, and Little Sister laughed in her heart as she
slipped the birch shoes on to his feet. "Now run, dear
feet," she whispered; "but do not outrun mine."

Up in his sleep leapt Fair Brother, for the dream of the
white birch had hold of him. A lady with a dark hood

and grey eyes full of the laughter of leaves beckoned him. Out he ran into the moonlight, and Little Sister laughed as she ran with him.

In a little while she called, "Do not outrun me, Fair Brother!" But he seemed not to hear her, for not a bit did he slacken the speed of his running.

Presently she cried again, "Rest with me a while, Fair Brother! Do not outrun me!" But Fair Brother's feet were fleet after their long idleness, and they only ran the faster. "Ah, ah!" she cried, all out of breath. "Come back to me when you have done running, Fair Brother." And as he disappeared among the trees, she cried after him, "How will you know the way, since you were never here before? Do not get lost in the wood, Fair Brother!"

She lay on the ground and listened, and could hear the white birch shoes carrying him away till all sound of them died.

When, next morning, he had not returned, she searched all day through the wood, calling his name.

"Where are you, Fair Brother? Where have you lost yourself?" she cried, but no voice answered her.

For a while she comforted her heart, saying, "He has not run all these years - no wonder he is still running. When he is tired he will return."

But days and weeks went by, and Fair Brother never came back to her. Every day she wandered searching for him, or sat at the door of the little wattled hut and cried.

Laurence Housman

One day she cried so much that the ground became quite wet with her tears. That night was the night of the full moon, but weary with grief she lay down and slept soundly, though outside the woods were bright.

In the middle of the night she started up, for she thought she heard somebody go by; and, surely, feet were running away in the distance. And when she looked out, there across the doorway was the print of the birch shoes on the ground she had made wet with her tears.

"Alas, alas!" cried Little Sister. "What have I done that he comes to the very door of our home and passes by, though the moon shines in and shows it him?"

After that she searched everywhere through the forest to discover the print of the birch shoes upon the ground. Here and there after rain she thought she could see traces, but never was she able to track them far.

Once more came the night of the full moon, and once more in the middle of the night Little Sister started up and heard feet running away in the distance. She called, but no answer came back to her.

So on the third full moon she waited, sitting in the door of the hut, and would not sleep.

"If he has been twice," she said to herself, "he will come again, and I shall see him. Ah, Fair Brother, Fair Brother, I have given you feet; why have you so used me?"

Presently she heard a sound of footsteps, and there came Fair Brother running towards her. She saw his face pale and ghostlike, yet he never looked at her, but ran past and on without stopping.

"Fair Brother, Fair Brother, wait for me; do not outrun me!" cried Little Sister; and was up in haste to be after him.

He ran fast, and would not stop; but she ran fast too, for her love would not let him go. Once she nearly had him by the hair, and once she caught him by the cloak; but in her hand it shredded and crumbled like a dry leaf; and still, though there was no breath left in her, she ran on.

And now she began to wonder, for Fair Brother was running the way that she knew well - towards the tree from which she had cut the two strips of bark. Her feet were failing her; she knew that she could run no more. Just as they came together in sight of the birch-tree Little Sister stumbled and fell.

She saw Fair Brother run on and strike with his hands and feet against the tree, and cry, "Oh, White Birch, White Birch, lift the latch up, or she will catch me!" And at once the tree opened its rind, and Fair Brother ran in.

"So," said Little Sister, "you are there, are you, Brother? I know, then, what I have done to you."

She went and laid her ear to the tree, and inside she could hear Fair Brother sobbing and crying. It sounded to her as if White Birch were beating him.

"Well, well, Fair Brother, she shall not beat you for long!" said Little Sister.

Laurence Housman

She went home and waited till the next full moon had come. Then, as soon as it was dark, she went along through the wood until she came to the place, and there she crept close to the white birch-tree and waited.

Presently she heard Fair Brother's voice come faintly out of the heart of the tree: "White Birch, it is the full moon and the hour in which Little Sister gave life to my feet. For one hour give me leave to go, that I may run home and look at her while she sleeps. I will not stop or speak, and I promise you that I will return."

Then she heard the voice of White Birch answer grudgingly: "It is her hour and I cannot hold you, therefore you may go. Only when you come again I will beat you."

Then the tree opened a little way, and Fair Brother ran out. He ran so quickly in his eager haste that Little Sister had not time to catch him, and she did not dare to call aloud. "I must make sure," she said to herself, "before he comes back. To-night White Birch will have to let him go."

So she gathered as many dry pieces of wood as she could find, and made them into a pile near at hand; and setting them alight, she soon had a brisk fire burning.

Before long she heard the sound of feet in the brush-wood, and there came Fair Brother, running as hard as he could go, with the breath sobbing in and out of his body.

Little Sister sprang out to meet him, but as soon as he saw her he beat with his hands and feet against the tree, crying, "White Birch, White Birch, lift the latch up, or she will catch me!"

But before the tree could open Little Sister had caught hold of the birch shoes, and pulled them off his feet, and running towards the fire she thrust them into the red heart of the embers.

The white birch shivered from head to foot, and broke into lamentable shrieks. The witch thrust her head out of the tree, crying, "Don't, don't! You are burning my skin! Oh, cruel! how you are burning me!"

"I have not burned you enough yet," cried Little Sister; and raking the burning sticks and faggots over the ground, she heaped them round the foot of the white birch-tree, whipping the flames to make them leap high.

The witch drew in her head, but inside she could be heard screaming. As the flames licked the white bark she cried, "Oh, my skin! You are burning my skin. My beautiful white skin will be covered with nothing but blisters. Do you know that you are ruining my complexion?"

But Little Sister said, "If I make you ugly you will not be able to show your face again to deceive the innocent, and to ruin hearts that were happy."

So she piled on sticks and faggots till the outside of the birch-tree was all black and scarred and covered with blisters, marks of which have remained to this day. And inside, the witch could be heard dancing time to the music of the flames, and crying because of her ruined complexion.

Laurence Housman

Then Little Sister stooped and took up Fair Brother in her arms. "You cannot walk now," she whispered, "I have taken away your feet; so I will carry you."

He was so starved and thin that he was not very heavy, and all the long way home Little Sister carried him in her arms. How happy they were, looking in each other's eyes by the clear light of the moon! "Can you ever be happy again in the old way?" asked Little Sister. "Shall you not want to run?"

"No," answered Fair Brother; "I shall never wish to run again. And as for the rest" - he stroked her head softly - "why, I can feel that your hair is growing - it is ever so long, and I can see the wind lifting it. White Birch has no hair of her own, but she has some that she wears, just the same colour as yours."

Choose from Thousands of 1stWorldLibrary Classics By

Adolphus WilliamWard
Aesop
Agatha Christie
Alexander Aaronsohn
Alexander Kielland
Alexandre Dumas
Alfred Gatty
Alfred Ollivant
Alice Duer Miller
Alice Turner Curtis
Alice Dunbar
Ambrose Bierce
Amelia E. Barr
Andrew Lang
Andrew McFarland Davis
Anna Sewell
Annie Besant
Annie Hamilton Donnell
Annie Payson Call
Anton Chekhov
Arnold Bennett
Arthur Conan Doyle
Arthur Ransome
Atticus
B. M. Bower
Basil King
Bayard Taylor
Ben Macomber
Booth Tarkington
Bram Stoker
C. Collodi
C. E. Orr
C. M. Ingleby
Carolyn Wells
Catherine Parr Traill
Charles A. Eastman
Charles Dickens
Charles Dudley Warner
Charles Farrar Browne
Charles Ives
Charles Kingsley
Charles Lathrop Pack
Charles Whibley
Charles Willing Beale
Charlotte M. Braeme
Charlotte M.Yonge
Clair W. Hayes
Clarence Day Jr.
Clarence E. Mulford

Clemence Housman
Confucius
Cornelis DeWitt Wilcox
Cyril Burleigh
D. H. Lawrence
Daniel Defoe
David Garnett
Don Carlos Janes
Donald Keyhole
Dorothy Kilner
Dougan Clark
E. Nesbit
E.P.Roe
E. Phillips Oppenheim
Edgar Allan Poe
Edgar Rice Burroughs
Edith Wharton
Edward J. O'Biren
John Cournos
Edwin L. Arnold
Eleanor Atkins
Elizabeth Cleghorn
Gaskell
Elizabeth Von Arnim
Ellem Key
Emily Dickinson
Erasmus W. Jones
Ernie Howard Pie
Ethel Turner
Ethel Watts Mumford
Eugenie Foa
Eugene Wood
Evelyn Everett-Green
Everard Cotes
F. J. Cross
Federick Austin Ogg
Ferdinand Ossendowski
Francis Bacon
Francis Darwin
Frances Hodgson Burnett
Frank Gee Patchin
Frank Harris
Frank Jewett Mather
Frank L. Packard
Frederick Trevor Hill
Frederick Winslow Taylor
Friedrich Kerst
Friedrich Nietzsche
Fyodor Dostoyevsky

Gabrielle E. Jackson
Garrett P. Serviss
Gaston Leroux
George Ade
Geroge Bernard Shaw
George Ebers
George Eliot
George MacDonald
George Orwell
George Tucker
George W. Cable
George Wharton James
Gertrude Atherton
Grace E. King
Grant Allen
Guillermo A. Sherwell
Gulielma Zollinger
Gustav Flaubert
H. A. Cody
H. B. Irving
H. G. Wells
H. H. Munro
H. Irving Hancock
H. Rider Haggard
H. W. C. Davis
Hamilton Wright Mabie
Hans Christian Andersen
Harold Avery
Harold McGrath
Harriet Beecher Stowe
Harry Houidini
Helent Hunt Jackson
Helen Nicolay
Hendy David Thoreau
Henrik Ibsen
Henry Adams
Henry Ford
Henry Frost
Henry James
Henry Jones Ford
Henry Seton Merriman
Henry Wadsworth
Longfellow
Henry W Longfellow
Herbert A. Giles
Herbert N. Casson
Herman Hesse
Homer
Honore De Balzac

Horace Walpole	Laurence Housman	Robert Lansing
Horatio Alger, Jr.	Leo Tolstoy	Robert Michael Ballantyne
Howard Pyle	Leonid Andreyev	Robert W. Chambers
Howard R. Garis	Lewis Carroll	Rosa Nouchette Carey
Hugh Lofting	Lilian Bell	Ross Kay
Hugh Walpole	Lloyd Osbourne	Rudyard Kipling
Humphry Ward	Louis Tracy	Samuel B. Allison
Ian Maclaren	Louisa May Alcott	Samuel Hopkins Adams
Israel Abrahams	Lucy Fitch Perkins	Sarah Bernhardt
J.G.Austin	Lucy Maud Montgomery	Selma Lagerlof
J. Henri Fabre	Lydia Miller Middleton	Sherwood Anderson
J. M. Barrie	Lyndon Orr	Sigmund Freud
J. Macdonald Oxley	M. H. Adams	Standish O'Grady
J. S. Knowles	Margaret E. Sangster	Stanley Weyman
J. Storer Clouston	Margaret Vandercook	Stella Benson
Jack London	Maria Edgeworth	Stephen Crane
Jacob Abbott	Maria Thompson Daviess	Stewart Edward White
James Allen	Mariano Azuela	Stijn Streuvels
James Lane Allen	Marion Polk Angellotti	Swami Abhedananda
James Andrews	Mark Overton	Swami Parmananda
James Baldwin	Mark Twain	T. S. Ackland
James DeMille	Mary Austin	The Princess Der Ling
James Joyce	Mary Cole	Thomas A. Janvier
James Oliver Curwood	Mary Rowlandson	Thomas A Kempis
James Oppenheim	Mary Wollstonecraft	Thomas Anderton
James Otis	Shelley	Thomas Bailey Aldrich
Jane Austen	Max Beerbohm	Thomas Bulfinch
Jens Peter Jacobsen	Myra Kelly	Thomas De Quincey
Jerome K. Jerome	Nathaniel Hawthrone	Thomas H. Huxley
John Burroughs	O. F. Walton	Thomas Hardy
John F. Kennedy	Oscar Wilde	Thomas More
John Gay	Owen Johnson	Thornton W. Burgess
John Glasworthy	P.G.Wodehouse	U. S. Grant
John Habberton	Paul and Mable Thorn	Valentine Williams
John Joy Bell	Paul G. Tomlinson	Victor Appleton
John Milton	Paul Severing	Virginia Woolf
John Philip Sousa	Peter B. Kyne	Walter Scott
Jonathan Swift	Plato	Washington Irving
Joseph Carey	R. Derby Holmes	Wilbur Lawton
Joseph Conrad	R. L. Stevenson	Wilkie Collins
Joseph Jacobs	Rabindranath Tagore	Willa Cather
Julian Hawthrone	Rahul Alvares	Willard F. Baker
Julies Vernes	Ralph Waldo Emmerson	William Makepeace
Justin Huntly McCarthy	Rene Descartes	Thackeray
Kakuzo Okakura	Rex E. Beach	William W. Walter
Kenneth Grahame	Richard Harding Davis	Winston Churchill
Kate Langley Bosher	Richard Jefferies	Yei Theodora Ozaki
L. A. Abbot	Robert Barr	Young E. Allison
L. T. Meade	Robert Frost	Zane Grey
L. Frank Baum	Robert Gordon Anderson	
Laura Lee Hope	Robert L. Drake	

www.ingramcontent.com/pod-product-compliance
Lightning Source LLC
Chambersburg PA
CBHW031844170626
46807CB00004B/1608